At His Feet

An Historical Fiction
Account of Ruth

At His Feet

An historical fiction account
of Ruth

Angela W. Buff

Word of His Mouth Publishers
Mooresboro, NC

All Scripture quotations are taken from the **King James Version** of the Bible.

ISBN: 978-1-941039-31-1
Printed in the United States of America
© 2023 Angela W. Buff

Word of His Mouth Publishers
Mooresboro, NC
www.wordofhismouth.com

Cover art by Chip Nuhrah

Table of Contents

Prologue

Rahab pulled the comb through her thick, black hair, watching her husband balance their young son on his knees. She never tired of this nightly ritual. She never tired of watching her husband and their child, whose hair and skin tone so matched his mother's, with eyes which so clearly matched his father's. It was the kindness deep inside those eyes that Rahab recognized every time she looked at her son. The kindness that had caught her attention the first time she saw Salmon and the same kindness that radiated from her husband's eyes every time she looked at him to this day.

"Around the city, we marched," Salmon continued in hushed tones. "One, two, three, four, five, six," he paused for effect and watched his young son's eyes grow wide, "seven times. On the seventh march, the priests raised their horns to their mouths, blew into them, the men gave a mighty shout, and…"

"De walls come tumblin' down!" Boaz finished in his two-year-old broken speech with a shout, raising his tiny arms into the air.

"That is right, my boy," Salmon smiled, pulling him to his chest in a fierce yet gentle hug. "The walls of Jericho fell, and across the broken walls, I rushed, found your mother, scooped her up onto the back of my horse, and ushered her quickly to safety," he finished. Boaz giggled in delight as his father tossed him onto his back and galloped him around the room.

Rahab smiled and joined her small family.

"Do not forget, it was I who first saved your father," Rahab reminded them as she took their son from her husband's back. "He had gotten himself into quite a situation earlier," she grinned sheepishly, glancing at her husband.

Salmon pretended to be thinking back before nodding slowly. "I suppose I must acknowledge that," he reluctantly, yet playfully, agreed. "But do not forget, I had indeed saved you once before even that."

"So, you had. But now," Rahab smiled as she laid their son onto his cot and tucked a thick fur around him, "it is time for someone to go to sleep." She bundled her beloved scarlet wrap into a pillow and offered it to the small boy, who snuggled it close to his face as he closed his heavy eyes. "Sleep sweet, my dear Boaz," she smiled as she placed a kiss on his brow and blew out the lamp.

Salmon stood waiting for his wife as she joined him. They faced their son, Salmon's arms circled about her waist, watching as their small boy slipped into a peaceful sleep.

"I know he is young, but already I pray he finds love as I did someday," Rahab spoke quietly, her head resting on his broad chest.

"He will," Salmon assured her. "In Jehovah's time, He will send a woman who will love and cherish Boaz as much as he does her."

"There is so much wrong in the world; how can you be so sure?" Rahab asked.

"Because everything was wrong in my world when Jehovah led me to you," he answered plainly. "I am sure Boaz will face uncertainty in his days, but we are teaching him that though there are uncertain times, we serve a certain God, and in Him, he will always find the answers for whatever it is he seeks."

"Such a wise husband I have," Rahab smiled, shifting in his arms to face him. "And I am certainly glad Jehovah brought you to my inn that day." She reached up to frame his cheek with her hand. "I love you, Salmon," she spoke quietly.

"And I love you, Rahab," he smiled in return. "Come, let us do as our young son and find our rest." With a final glance to assure her son's comfort, Rahab followed her husband to their chambers. Salmon fell asleep quickly, but Rahab took her time before drifting off. Instead, she lay content in her husband's arms, thanking God for all He had delivered her from. She thanked Him for all He had given her since; for the promise that He alone held her future, and for the peace He promised could always be found when she sought His will and His comfort at His feet.

Many Years Later

Chapter One

Ruth sat on the ground, gentle tears silently trailing her face. She had been in this spot for hours, but she could not pull herself away. Before her lay the graves of the three men who had been the most important people in her world, her father-in-law, her brother-in-law, and, most devastatingly, her husband. It had been months since it had happened, but the pain was as fresh as if it were just yesterday. She remembered the smile he had tossed back at her over his shoulder as he walked away that fateful day and how much it had reminded her of the first time she had seen him. A sob caught in her throat, and fresh tears burned her eyes as memories of the first time she met Mahlon played in her mind.

His father, Elimelech, had made the choice to leave their home in Bethlehem-Judea. With him, he had brought his wife, Naomi, and their two sons, Mahlon and Chilion, here to Moab. They had come seeking a place in which they could visit to escape the famine that had overtaken their land.

"We are only here for a little time," Elimelech had often said, "for we shall return home soon." Time and again, he had expressed that they were only sojourning here, adamant that their home was in Bethlehem and their stay in Moab would be brief. "We just needed to escape the destitution," he had explained, "for only a little while."

And you came here to Moab? Ruth remembered thinking to herself. She had never fully understood Elimelech's thinking when it came to bringing his family across the river to her land, though out of respect for him, she would never voice her questions aloud. She had heard stories of the famine in Israel. She knew food had gotten scarce and was hard to come by there, and no doubt, Elimelech had feared for his family and their safety, but to bring them to this land, the land of Moab, this land of darkness and sorrow? The people of Israel were supposed to have nothing to do with the Moabites, yet Elimelech had brought his family into the midst of them. Though his plan was to stay for only a little while, his reasoning was still puzzling to her.

Ruth thought again of the first time she had crossed paths with the family. She had been in town gathering water when Elimelech approached her, asking if she would share the water she drew. He asked not for himself but for his wife. Ruth remembered the way he had looked at Naomi, his eyes brimming with such concern and compassion for her well-being. The man genuinely cared for his wife and sought her comfort. Ruth secretly hoped then that she would find someone who would look at her that way. It was an unusual occurrence to find such care in the land of Moab.

Ruth knew of the famine in the neighboring city and realized that these Israelites must have been some of the most desperate in their land in order for them to feel the need to travel to Moab. The lifestyle in Moab was different, their culture was different, but most of all, their gods were different. Ruth drew water not only for his wife that day but for Elimelech and his sons as well. Though she was a Moabitess, she knew sadness and desperation when she saw it and felt that kindness reached far beyond the boundaries of cultural differences.

She had drawn water for the family that day and for Mahlon when he returned the day after, and the day after that, and the day after that, always being rewarded with a smile he would toss to her as he walked away.

For weeks Mahlon continued to meet her by the well, and as he drank the water she drew, he would tell her stories of his life in Bethlehem-Judea before the famine. It was through those stories he shared with her that he told her of the God of his people and how different his God was from the god Chemosh, which was the god Ruth had been taught to worship in Moab. Mahlon told her not only of how Jehovah God had protected his own family through the years but of men named Noah and Moses and the miraculous ways He had saved them from a flood, used them to free slaves, and protected them from the harsh wilderness. Ruth remembered hearing tales of that as a child, but Mahlon brought them to life as he explained how his people, the Jews, had wandered the desert for forty years, seeking the Promised Land.

Her favorite story, however, was of Mahlon's ancestor, Abraham, and how God had provided a sacrifice for Abraham when he felt he had no choice but to sacrifice his own son as an offering to their God. God had delivered Abraham's son, Isaac, by sending a ram to be the sacrifice required. Ruth told Mahlon of events she had witnessed that had torn her heart in two, rituals which had ended in mothers laying their newborn babies in the stone hands of their god Chemosh, only to burn them alive in sacrifice to their god.

Their conversations grew much more personal and intense in the following months, and Ruth noticed that Mahlon's mother, Naomi, began to accompany him to the well. At first, Ruth thought Naomi was coming to keep conversations between herself and Mahlon to a minimum; after all, she was a Moabite and he an Israelite, but as time passed, her relationship with Naomi began to grow, and Ruth realized the older woman simply had a desire to see her come to know the same Jehovah God she and her family served. It also had not escaped Naomi's attention that her other son, Chilion, had taken an interest in Orpah, another beautiful Moabitess who lived near the center of town. Her family was not quite as accepting of their out-of-town visitors, and Orpah was far less receptive to hearing of the God of Israel, though she was very receptive to Chilion and his interest in her.

Time passed quickly, and Elimelech's plan to visit for "a little while" became a month, and then six months, and then a year, before Elimelech had taken ill. The sickness consumed him, and in a very short time, he was past not only the ability to travel back home to Bethlehem but beyond hope of recovery. With heavy hearts, they had buried Elimelech in a land that was not his home, a foreign land beyond the borders of Bethlehem-Judea, where he had always planned to return. His visit to Moab, where he had planned to simply sojourn for "just a little while," had become his final destination.

Mahlon took Ruth to be his wife soon after, not only for himself but also to serve as a companion to his mother. Shortly thereafter, Chilion and Orpah had wed, and though the relationship between the family and Orpah's was somewhat strained, they remained in Moab, making a life for themselves and caring for Naomi as best they could for the past ten years; until now.

As the events of the past few weeks came back to her mind, Ruth pushed herself up from her husband's grave and stood gazing at the mountains. Those mountains, which protected the solemn graves from the sun, were the very mountains that had so harshly taken her husband from her. She was not clear on exactly what had happened, only that Mahlon and Chilion had left their home to hunt, failing to return. The women's worst fears were confirmed when a neighbor arrived two days later, the bodies of both Mahlon and Chilion draped over the backs of their own animals. It appeared Chilion had fallen into a ravine, and in Mahlon's attempt to rescue him, he had fallen in as well. The neighbor assured them it seemed from their wounds that the men had died on impact. He had carefully climbed into the ravine himself, out of respect for the widows, to perform the arduous task of retrieving the bodies.

Ruth had thought Naomi had been broken the day they had buried Elimelech, but never had she seen the woman so torn as the day she buried both of her sons, one on either side of her husband. All of the trust and faith she had shown in Jehovah God for countless years seemed to be wavering as she continued to sink deeper and deeper into a dark depression. Orpah did nothing but sit and stare out the window in their front room. She had never taken easily to assisting with daily chores and with the running of the house, but she had always been pleasant company. Yet, since the death of Chilion, she desired nothing and offered nothing, regardless of how much she realized Naomi needed to draw from the strength of her daughters-in-law. Orpah simply had no strength to give.

The setting sun behind the mountain reminded Ruth that her time alone today was done. She wiped the tears from her face with the hem of her garment and began the short walk back into the home she now shared with two other widows. She could not allow Orpah and Naomi to see that she had been upset again. She must remain strong, not strong for just herself, but strong enough for all three of them.

With a silent promise to return to the grave tomorrow, she said a quick prayer to the God she had come to love so deeply and rely on so desperately. Ruth knew the only way she would survive was by leaning on that very God, the God that her husband had taught her to serve, the God of Israel.

Chapter Two

Naomi sat alone in the darkening room. She watched Ruth through her window which faced the mountains, the sky bursting with the colors of the setting sun. At one time, Naomi would have cherished the beauty of it. Early evening used to be her favorite time of day. As the day began to wane and the light began to fade, her boys would begin making their way indoors. Elimelech would do his best to be by her side before darkness descended upon them and the last beam of the sun had shone until morning. He would wrap his arms around her, regardless of who was near, and thank God for another day with his family. Her boys would follow, kissing their mother on the cheek as they passed, their gentle hugs embracing both her body and soul. Before, back when they were in Bethlehem.

Their family had been a close one, and those memories were cherished, but the sadness they brought with them now was very real. Because of these memories, Naomi now dreaded the evening. Yet truthfully, she dreaded it no more than she dreaded morning, or noon, or the middle of the night, or any other time of the day.

Why had he brought them here? What had possessed Elimelech to believe Moab was a wise decision? Naomi allowed her mind to wander again back to Bethlehem before the famine. She remembered as far back as when Elimelech had asked for her hand and had taken her as his wife in their youth. She remembered when God had allowed her to give Elimelech not one son, but two, and the pride he had in each of his boys. In the beginning, their life in Bethlehem was good. Elimelech was a good provider, a good father, and a wonderful husband. They had no need for anything, either physically or mentally. They were a hardworking, strong, well-loved family. Because of this, the townspeople not only respected Elimelech but sought him out for advice and counsel. "Elimelech will know what to do," she had heard them say, "Let us ask Elimelech his opinion on the matter." His advice and the decisions he had made had always been wise. Up until he made the decision to come to Moab.

Times had changed, and things had grown very bleak in their homeland of Bethlehem. The country was without a ruler, and men began ruling themselves, every man doing that which was right in his own eyes. This had led to so much greed and immorality that Elimelech rarely allowed Naomi to venture from their own home, much less into town. He and the boys did any business that was necessary while she stayed inside and tended to things there. Neighbors were no longer dear friends, and friends were scarce to be found.

Judgment had fallen upon their people. Crops stopped producing, and meat was becoming hard to find. It had become a bleak life, but it was a life in which she still had her husband and her sons, and she would trade that now for all the food in the world. Elimelech had thought he had kept the obvious hidden from Naomi, but she knew of the despair in their land.

Naomi shook her head as the conversation played again in her mind. She had never fully questioned Elimelech, though she had expressed her reservations. She remembered every word they exchanged over the matter as clearly as if it had taken place just yesterday.

"I believe a journey is in order," he had begun one night as they finished their small evening meal and the boys had gone outside to finish their chores.

"A journey?" she questioned, her interest piqued.

"Yes," he continued. "I am concerned, Naomi," he began as he confided in her. "Things are not improving here as I had hoped. In fact, they are continuing to worsen. People are hardening themselves more and more against all things good. Frustration continues to mount among our people, among our neighbors even, and I fear there is coming a time in which our closest friends will become our bitter enemies."

"Elimelech, has something happened?" she had asked, fear creeping into her voice.

"No, no, not yet," he spoke softly, patting her hand with his own to calm her, "I just sense an uneasiness in the people and in myself. Food is becoming more and more scarce and each man is accusing the other of taking more than his share, and in truth, some of them are. They are scared, Naomi, but instead of turning to God as I prayed they would, I feel their tension building. Perhaps if we could pull ourselves away from the center of it all for just a little while, I could collect my thoughts and determine a way to help our people. I have heard that in Moab, there is plenty of bread and meat, and…" his voice trailed off as he saw the look crossing her face.

"And wickedness and sin," she injected. "Moab? Elimelech, you cannot be serious. Why would you want to journey to such a land? They are a horrid and desolate people. Why would you even consider dwelling there? Nothing good ever comes from the land of Moab," she began to laugh until she saw the seriousness on his face and stopped abruptly. "Elimelech, can you be serious?" she asked.

His features were strained, and Naomi could feel the tension in his mood before he spoke. "Nothing good is coming from Bethlehem right now either, Naomi," he had argued. "The people here are becoming as horrid and desolate as the Moabites. And, I do not plan for us to dwell in Moab, only to sojourn there for a little time. Just long enough for some of the uneasiness to leave my bones and for some bread and meat to completely fill our stomachs. I just long to take a little break from this famine, from this despair, and to give the people here time to settle down a bit."

"But we are not starving yet, Elimelech," she began, "we have food..."

"Yet, Naomi," he interrupted, "we are not starving, yet!" he emphasized the word while quickly rising from his seat. "But how long will we wait? Until our growing sons come to us hungry and asking for food? Until you look at me and say the barrel is empty and the meal is gone? I heard you scrape the bottom of that barrel just today! Will we wait until I come home empty-handed and tell you there is no meat to be found? Naomi, the crops are not producing a portion of what they normally do. Our harvest will be bleak if we gather any at all. People are passing their own judgment on one another daily, and there is fighting and killing in these very streets, the streets of Bethlehem. There is nothing to stay here for!" he finished.

Naomi could not stop the tear that escaped her eye as the harshness of reality set in. Not only the reality of their situation, but also the reality that Elimelech was serious. The shock of what he was saying, yet of the truth she knew his words contained, were overwhelming.

"But Elimelech, this is home," she spoke softly, "we have raised our boys here. We have built our life here; our friends and family, they are all here. We have always warned our sons of

Moab, Elimelech, and now you plan to take us all there? I do not understand the wisdom in that."

Elimelech knelt in front of her where she sat, placing his hands on her knees. "I am not speaking of living there, Naomi, only taking a short journey there. We will go to Moab, just for a little while, and then return here, back to our home. Hopefully, in that short span of time while we are away, things will improve here. We will get our fill of bread and meat there, our people will turn back to our God here, and when we return to Bethlehem, we will return to the home we remember, the home we love. Our home the way it was before the famine. I fear that continuing here among these people as we are now will lead to our certain destruction."

Naomi had seen that look in his eyes before. It was a look of determination. His mind was made up. For whatever reason, he was convinced they should travel to Moab, and nothing she could do or say would convince him otherwise. She placed her hand on the side of his face and said the only words she knew to say.

"When do we leave?" Four simple words she had been so foolish as to utter, four simple words that had completely changed her life.

And so they had. They left everything in Bethlehem, except what few things they could carry, and came to Moab. *Just for a little while,* she remembered. Naomi shook her head as tears began to slide along her withered cheeks. If she had only put him off for a little longer and encouraged him to pray and seek Jehovah's will in the matter, he may still be with her now, but no. She had said the words and sealed their fate. *When do we leave?*

Fresh tears burned her eyes. Now Elimelech would never leave this God-forsaken country, he, or Mahlon, or Chilion. Elimelech's diversion had become their final destiny. Now all Naomi had left was herself and two Moabite daughters-in-law who were as broken and empty as she. Why had she ever uttered those four words, "W*hen do we leave?*" Everything had been left behind in Bethlehem, and now she had nothing, nor did she want anything.

Watching her daughter-in-law make her way back inside, she knew how unfair she was being to the two women who had become her only family. She had been so consumed by her own grief she had offered no comfort to the younger women of her household. But how could she? She could barely summon the strength to rise each morning and would not bother to were it not for Ruth.

Ruth had attempted, through her own grief, to carry on with daily life, though Naomi and Orpah barely functioned. Each of the women had to mourn in their own way, but Naomi knew of the three of them, it was Ruth's strength that had given her the courage to wake each morning. Were it not for Ruth, Naomi would not bother to rise and dress herself each day. Ruth did the cooking; otherwise, Naomi would not bother to eat. Ruth did the cleaning, went into town when needed, drew the water, and cared for what little livestock they had. Ruth did it all.

She continually attempted to encourage Naomi and Orpah by reminding them of the faith Naomi's family had taught her of. She tried to be a help, especially to the older woman, but what Ruth did not realize was that she, herself, was a constant reminder of all that Naomi had lost. Every time she looked at Ruth, she saw the beautiful maiden at the well they had first met when they came to Moab. Every time she looked at Ruth, she heard Mahlon's laughter fill the room as they talked of the maiden by the well before he brought her to be his wife. Yes, Ruth was a wonderful addition to their family, but it didn't change the fact that Ruth had been Mahlon's wife and that Ruth was a Moabitess.

Naomi turned from the window to see Orpah asleep on the cot she had shared with Chilion just a few weeks before. Orpah, who still had her doubts about the God her husband and his family had served, now questioned how they could continue to believe in a God who would take all the men from their home, leaving them desperate and alone. Naomi would never admit aloud her own questions on that matter. However, two Moabite women had joined their family and though very different, they all shared a close relationship, or at least they had. Now they shared nothing but grief.

When do we leave? The words echoed over again in Naomi's mind. Were she ever to consider returning to Bethlehem, how would her friends back home react to her bringing two Moabite women with her? They would take no time to discover the beauty beyond their physical appearance before casting judgment on them all. God had been very direct in his instructions to keep the two cultures separate, and not only had Naomi and Elimelech left Bethlehem to come to Moab, they had also allowed two Moabite women to join their family. They had directly gone against the God that they had so often encouraged others to believe and trust in.

But what did it matter? It was not as if she had a home in Bethlehem to return to. Elimelech's promise of "just a little while" had turned into over twelve years in Moab. At one time, their family had been among the most respected and prominent in their village, but now, their names were probably never mentioned, their home probably in ruins, and their faces just a memory to those they had once considered close friends.

Naomi felt as if her world were crashing around her all over again. She had left everything, she had lost everything, and regardless of where she was, nothing would ever be the same. "Lord, where are you," she cried to herself. "Have you left me, too?" she sobbed.

As if He were standing in her presence, Naomi felt a presence she had not felt in years creep into her heart. "I have not left you, Naomi," she felt Him whisper. "You have left me."

Naomi lifted her head, tears streaming down her withered cheeks. How true were those words? They were as clear to her as if they had been audibly spoken, and though there was silence in the room, Naomi knew those words had come to her from God Himself. He had not left her. She had turned from Him. When she and Elimelech left Bethlehem, God had not stayed behind there; they had left Him behind there. They had walked away from Him, and though their intentions had not been to turn from God, that is exactly what they had done. They had walked out of His will and into their own. They had walked out of His land and into a land of darkness. They were trying to fix something that was not theirs to fix. Their faith should have been stronger; they had acted on fear instead of relying on the wisdom that God would continue to provide for them. In truth, He had never stopped providing for them in Bethlehem. It was their own lack of faith with which they were dealing. They had taken their eyes off of the God they had taught their sons to serve and instead focused on the circumstances surrounding them. In doing so, they allowed "what ifs" to become their reality and their faith to become their fear.

Darkness now loomed outside her window, and Naomi felt that darkness to the depths of her soul. She covered her face with her hands and sobbed, pleading with her God, the same God of her fathers, the same God of her family, and the same God of Bethlehem to forgive her. To forgive her for her lack of faith, to forgive her for her lack of wisdom, and to forgive her for ever doubting His love for her.

But would He even hear her prayer in this God-forsaken land? He would not return her husband or her sons from their graves. He would not honor her for forsaking Him and coming to Moab, specifically against His instructions, even though it was her husband who had encouraged her to do so. She could not lay all the blame at Elimelech's feet, however; she had an equal part in their sin. She had spoken the words, *When do we leave.*

When she finished her prayer, though the house was quiet, the sound of loneliness seemed to whirl around her. She covered her ears to escape the sound of nothing. Her shoulders still felt the weight of her burdens, but her eyes were swollen, and her heart was tired. She was not certain that God would forgive her, she wasn't sure she was in the proper mindset to truly seek that forgiveness, but would He possibly at least have mercy on her?

What to do now? She had attempted to ask for God's forgiveness, but her heart was still consumed with bitterness. He had taken everything from her because of their sin. She wiped her eyes once more and slowly rose from her place at the window, stretching her back. She could do nothing but wait.

She would wait and pray for direction from God, if He would supply any, as she and Elimelech should have done many years ago before they left their home. Acting in haste of their own volition had gotten them into this mess years ago, and Naomi would not repeat that tragic mistake again. She would do her best to cope, continue to seek God's forgiveness, and continue to pray for strength to get through each day. She would not bother to pray for peace and comfort in her own time of sorrow, she deserved to be miserable, but she would attempt to pray for peace for her daughters-in-law. She had not been for them what she should be, and if God would not honor her request for her own forgiveness, perhaps He would deal more kindly with her if she were to at least attempt to encourage them.

She turned toward the door as she saw Ruth enter their home slowly. She watched as her daughter-in-law quietly closed the door behind herself and wiped a lonely tear, which had escaped her eye, from off her cheek. Even through the darkness, Naomi recognized the despair on Ruth's beautiful face though Ruth tried so desperately to mask it. Unnoticed, Naomi looked to the cot where Orpah lay, where she always lay, completely broken. Naomi closed her eyes and sank back into her chair once again, a fresh torrent of tears burning behind her eyes. How could she attempt to encourage these women when she could not even summon the strength to cross the room? What was the use in trying? How could she?

Chapter Three

Ruth finally succeeded in coaxing Naomi outdoors the next day when the sun was at its highest. The weather was pleasant, and she knew a walk would do them both good. Orpah, however, refused to come, politely rejecting Ruth's plea and turning back to face her dark room, attempting to find comfort in her own solitude as she so often did.

The two ladies who walked were silent as they traveled the lonely path toward town. Their pace was slow, and Ruth had allowed Naomi her solitude, content with the fact that she was outside, stretching her legs. They had gone a far distance before Naomi stopped and began to speak. Her voice was broken and low, and Ruth had to listen closely to make out the words.

"Ruth, I owe you an apology," she began slowly, "for the way I have handled myself over the death of my boys."

"You owe me nothing," Ruth quickly answered. "It has been an incredibly difficult time for all of us."

"True," Naomi continued, "but you have handled this with far more grace and faith than I could have ever hoped to. I am supposed to be your teacher when it comes to matters of our faith, but I must admit, you have shamed me as of late," she continued as she brushed away a tear that had escaped her eye.

"I have lost a husband, Naomi. You have lost an entire family. I am sure the God of Israel understands that you are heartbroken and grieving." Ruth steadied her mother-in-law with a hand to her elbow as she slowly resumed her pace, and the older woman began to speak again.

"I had hoped Orpah would have embraced our faith as you have, yet I realize I have been a poor teacher. Regardless, I fear these tragedies have only driven a deeper wedge into her faltering beliefs."

"When you were raised and taught to believe in and worship stone idols as gods, it is not easy to believe in something you cannot visibly see," Ruth admitted, "but as I told Mahlon before, there was an uneasiness in my heart even before I met your family, which I cannot explain."

"How so?" Naomi questioned, her curiosity obvious.

"Even as a child, I never understood the ways of the gods of my people," Ruth began. "I am not sure Orpah had ever questioned those teachings. I feel she just accepted them because it was what was expected of her, but I had always harbored an uneasy feeling about the Moabite religion."

"Such as?" Naomi questioned, encouraging Ruth to continue.

"I never understood why we should be worshipping someone, or something, with such harsh demands and rituals as Chemosh? He is just a statue which our ancestors fashioned and created with their own hands. Yet this statue, Chemosh, supposedly demands the sacrifice of newborn babies. Babies that are often the result of the unethical practices that he, too, has supposedly commanded. I cannot comprehend that. First, how does a statue, which is nothing more than a stone created from one's hand, command anything of anyone? The figure does not live nor breathe, yet he has commands and requirements of us? And we are to bow down and worship that same figure which was created by man?" Ruth shook her head, still confused over the monstrosity of it all. "I now feel that doubt I experienced was God preparing my heart for acceptance of Him," she continued, "for the time I met Mahlon, and he told me of Jehovah's goodness and mercy. I believe it grieved Mahlon at times that I did not bear him a child, though he would never admit it, but I tried to believe that maybe it was for the best since everyone around us continues to practice the Moabite religion. After all, my marriage to an Israelite did not bode well with some."

"You speak with wisdom, Ruth, but I can sense your sadness over your barrenness."

Ruth stopped once again and faced her mother-in-law. She contemplated her next words before she spoke them. She had secretly hoped she would remain barren and had often felt selfish for doing so, for she knew of Mahlon's desire for children. But she had a good reason for her selfish desire. She was a Moabite, regardless of her newfound beliefs, and her husband was an Israelite. That was something the people of Moab did not appreciate. Her fear had always been of giving Mahlon a child, only to have that child stolen from them by a Moabite trying to prove a point, who would then spitefully sacrifice their child to the pagan God her people worshiped. After all, an Israeli child would not have been accepted in her land, even if the mother were a local. The Moabite people were loyal to Chemosh, and they were not above doing whatever they deemed necessary to satisfy their god. Ruth would have accepted being barren forever before she could have accepted having to live with the thought of her child becoming a sacrifice to a man-made god.

Mahlon's words on the matter came back to her now, and those were the words she chose to share with Naomi.

"As Mahlon told me often, it is Jehovah God who creates life. We are simply the vessels He uses to carry it. If He had intended for me to have a child, I would have. Besides, what shape would we have been in now had we children to tend to as well as ourselves?" Ruth spoke truthfully.

"Yes, it is Jehovah God who gives life," Naomi began, "and it is He who takes life as well," she finished quietly. She sighed deeply and placed a withered hand on Ruth's cheek. "And we, regardless of how little sense we can make from it, must accept that."

Ruth and Naomi continued their walk in silence then, both becoming aware of a small caravan of travelers approaching them. It was not unusual for caravans to come through as they moved from city to city; people seldom traveled alone through Moab. As they drew closer, Ruth noticed Naomi pause, focusing attentively on the approaching company. One person, in particular, seemed to have caught her attention. Naomi squinted her eyes, and a moment later, her face began to soften.

"Miriam?" she spoke softly, almost to herself.

"Who?" Ruth asked, scanning the crowd, though she recognized no locals from the village among them.

As the caravan continued past, the woman Naomi had taken an interest in seemed to focus on Naomi. She stopped as she approached and looked carefully into her face. "Naomi?" she questioned.

"Miriam!" Naomi acknowledged. "It is you!"

The two ladies embraced and seemed genuinely pleased to see one another. Ruth stood back but remained watchful as the remaining travelers took the opportunity to rest while the ladies spoke.

"Naomi, I cannot believe it is you! I never would have recognized you had you not noticed me first! So often, I have grieved that Elimelech took you away from our village! I feared the worst when you did not return quickly as he promised, yet here you are!" She hugged her friend again and Ruth felt the sincerity of the conversation.

"Miriam, you look wonderful!" Naomi spoke almost as quickly, "I cannot believe how well you look with all of the troubles in Bethlehem! Have things gotten so bad that you, too, have escaped to Moab?" Naomi questioned honestly.

"Escaped?" Miriam asked, backing away but not letting go of her friend. "Oh, Naomi, have you not heard? There is no need to escape our land! The famine is over! Jehovah is once again blessing our Bethlehem-Judea! The rains have returned and the fields are full with the promise of a bountiful harvest this year! Our people are singing and praising as His blessings reign upon us once again! Enemies are once again friends. We are only quickly passing through this horrid place. It is the quickest way back and we cannot get home quickly enough! Where is Elimelech, and who is this lovely woman with you?" Miriam inquired, finally looking at Ruth, who was standing quietly nearby.

"This is my daughter-in-law, Ruth," Naomi replied, avoiding the question regarding Elimelech. Ruth took notice and moved closer to her mother-in-law.

"Daughter-in-law?" Miriam questioned, pulling quickly away from Naomi. Their brace was so quickly broken that the older woman almost stumbled. Ruth recognized the surprise in their companions' voice as an unwelcome one. The smile that had toyed on Naomi's lips quickly fell completely away as Miriam continued, her voice low yet sure. "I assumed she was a servant. One of your sons has married a Moabite?" she questioned quietly and slowly. Ruth had no trouble hearing the comment, nor the disgust that dripped from every word.

"Both of my sons have taken a Moabite for their wife," Naomi spoke with surety, holding her head high. "And they chose well," she finished looking at Ruth.

Ruth accepted the olive branch, though it had come from her mother-in-law and not Miriam.

"I am Ruth," she spoke humbly, stepping up to stand beside Naomi. "It is a pleasure to meet a friend of Naomi's."

"Yes, well," Miriam stammered as if the realization was too much for her to endure. "Well, my, my, fellow travelers are ready to proceed I do believe… and I hate, I hate, to leave in haste Naomi," she spoke quickly as she backed away almost tripping over her own feet, "but I really should not be keeping everyone. It was a sincere pleasure to see you again, Naomi. Give my best to Elimelech and your sons," she finished as she quickly walked away. Miriam attempted to shield her eyes as if even daring to look back would cause her to turn into a pillar of salt.

Naomi watched the lady as she approached her companions, waving eagerly in encouragement for them to continue their journey quickly. Miriam honestly felt she could not escape their presence fast enough. Ruth watched for Naomi's response to her friend's reaction. Nothing showed on her face as she watched the departure. She just stared quietly as they began to move away.

"I am sorry that your friend was in such a haste to leave that you did not have a chance to tell her about Elimelech," Ruth spoke truthfully. Naomi waved the comment away as she watched the small caravan depart, Miriam among them now and whispering to another lady in the company. "And I am sorry her reaction to me was not as pleasant as you would have hoped," Ruth finished. Naomi continued to watch them depart as the lady to whom Miriam directly spoke dared a quick glance of shock over her shoulder in the direction of Ruth.

Naomi broke her gaze at the departing company and looked straight into Ruth's eyes. "Do not ever apologize for being who you are, Ruth," she spoke firmly. "There is not a woman in all the world who could have gone through what you have gone through and retained the strength, spirit, and gentleness you show every day. There is no other in the whole world that I would rather have in my family, including anyone in Bethlehem-Judea. I do wish the circumstances could have been different, but Mahlon did well when choosing a wife. It is not your fault you were born a Moabite, nor that we came here and disrupted your world." Ruth hugged her mother-in-law with such fierceness she was worried she would hurt her. She softened her grasp but remained in the embrace until Naomi let her go. She could not love this woman more if she were her own flesh and blood.

Ruth felt tears sting her eyes but quickly blinked them away. She instead focused on her mother-in-law's face.

"I know that look," Ruth began as she saw a faraway expression suddenly cross Naomi's features. "Something is playing on your mind."

"Yes," Naomi admitted, a small smile playing at the edges of her mouth but never blooming. "It was something Miriam said," Naomi started, her voice trailing off.

"About thinking I was your servant?" Ruth laughed in an attempt to lighten the mood.

"No, not that," Naomi continued first looking at Ruth and then in the direction the caravan had gone. "She was always rather small-minded," Naomi spoke plainly, and Ruth giggled at the bluntness of her words. "It is what she said about Bethlehem," Naomi continued. "Miriam said the famine has left the land, Ruth. That God is again blessing His people there, and enemies had become friends once again. I wonder…" Naomi's voice trailed away once again.

"You wonder what, Naomi?" Ruth asked moving closer to her mother-in-law. Naomi looked at Ruth, tears sparkling again in her clouded eyes.

"I wonder," she began honestly, "if I am up to the journey."

"I am sorry," Ruth apologized, taking Naomi's arm and turning back toward their home. "We have gone a bit further than I intended, but I was enjoying our time so much," she continued. "I will get you home. Maybe we should sit a moment first before we begin our walk back?"

"No," Naomi surprised her, stopping and looking intently into her eyes. "I am not speaking of our walk to our home here in Moab. I am speaking of *my* home, Ruth. I wonder if I am up to the journey back to Bethlehem. I want to go home."

Ruth did not expect that announcement. Nor did she expect the way her heart skipped a beat in her chest at the very thought of it.

Chapter Four

A week had passed, and nothing more had been said about Naomi's declaration to Ruth that she desired to return home. Ruth hoped that it had just been the result of seeing her friend from Bethlehem that had triggered the emotion from Naomi, but something in the back of Ruth's mind continued to contemplate the thought of Naomi returning back there.

Question after question had played in her mind, especially tonight, and she dwelled on those questions as she cleaned up from the evening meal. Would the people in Bethlehem accept Naomi's return? It had been over ten years since Elimelech had left Bethlehem and brought his family to Moab. Did Naomi have a home to return to? The home she had left behind was surely in ruins if no one had tended to it, and if someone had taken the responsibility of tending to the home, had they claimed it as their own? It was clear that Miriam had not accepted Ruth as a part of Naomi's family; how would the other people of Bethlehem react to her Moabite daughter-in-law, especially when she arrived there without a husband? Would she be welcomed at all? Would she even be allowed to settle there as a Moabite in a foreign land? And then the ultimate question, the one that tarried the longest in her mind and that she feared the most was would Naomi be capable of completing the journey? She was many years older than when she had made the journey before, and she had lost so much during her time in Moab. The sorrow she carried with her now weighed far more than the fear she had shouldered during her first journey across the desert, and this time, there would be no men to help and protect her along the way.

Ruth shook her head to clear her confusion. There were too many questions to even begin to seriously consider the possibility of return, yet the nagging feeling continued that maybe it was what should be done. Ruth knew that the bitterness Naomi faced would only continue to worsen in Moab. Though her shoulders did not seem to slump quite as low, there was still a deep sadness in her eyes that burned to her soul, and the smile she had once been so eager to share never graced her face. Naomi's heart was broken, and her spirit had been quenched.

Then there was Orpah. No matter how much Ruth attempted to carry on, despite her own loss, Orpah continued to grieve, focused solely on her own sorrow. She did nothing, said nothing, and attended to nothing. She barely attended to her own needs, much less to that of the home or to the two other women who shared it with her. Perhaps a change of scenery would do them all good; a new beginning in a place away from Moab and away from the constant reminders of all they had lost. And if God was truly blessing in Bethlehem again, would Naomi be blessed there with peace as well? Or would the changes that were sure to have taken place among her people over the past decade be too much for the elderly woman to endure?

Regardless of her own feelings and confused thoughts on the matter, Ruth decided that until Naomi mentioned it again, she would not remind her mother-in-law of her declaration. She felt certain the issue would resurface, but until it did, Moab was her home. It was certainly far from perfect, but it was all she knew, and it was what she was used to. She would simply seek to find strength in the God Mahlon had taught her of, the God she had accepted and was determined to serve, to get herself and the ladies in her care through each day.

Ruth sighed as she finished her chores, her thoughts now going back to meals she had shared with her husband in times past. The evening meal used to be filled with fellowship and laughter, the food they consumed being only a part of what filled them. The companionship they had all shared at the table when the men were still with them had filled their soul, and that is what had left them all content and satisfied at the end of the day. How she missed her husband, but she could not allow her companions to see her struggle. She blinked back the tears, refusing to allow them to fall. Each time she left the table now she felt emptier than when she had approached it. She did not even taste the food anymore. Eating was simply a part of surviving. No meal was any different than the other, each one bleak and sad. She truthfully did not know how much longer she could continue to be the only strength in this family of widows she was now a part of. As if Naomi had read her mind, she broke the silence.

"I would like to speak with the two of you," she said with certainty looking at each of her daughters-in-law. Ruth crossed the room and took a seat beside Naomi. The confident look on her mother-in-law's face sent a shiver racing up her spine. Ruth quickly realized the very conversation she had been anticipating, yet fearing, was about to take place. Orpah turned in her seat across from them to better face the older woman, though Ruth was not sure she was even seeing her. Orpha's eyes, which were once so vibrant and would dance in the light, were now hard as stone. Her delicate, fair skin that had once been the envy of even Ruth was now pale and brittle. Bitterness may have consumed Naomi, but it was a harsh coldness that had taken over Orpah. There was nothing left of her physically or mentally that had been untouched. Her heart had been hardened by her grief.

"I want to first offer an apology to the both of you," Naomi began. She held up her hand indicating her desire for silence as Ruth shifted to interrupt her. "Let me speak," Naomi instructed. Ruth looked to her own hands where she held them tightly in her lap and bit her tongue, stopping herself from defending the frail woman seated beside her. She hated when Naomi took responsibility for her grief. Ignoring Ruth's discomfort, the woman continued.

"Before Elimelech passed, we had been quite diligent in teaching the two of you the ways of our faith. We wanted you to witness us not only speaking of our faith but of living it as well. Elimelech mentioned to me on one occasion that perhaps the two of you were our very purpose for coming to Moab. It eased his conscience regarding his disobedience in doing so anyway. You may have never heard of the goodness of our God were it not for our visit here, and who knows, God can and will bring good out of any situation He desires to, even in those situations when we have walked away from Him." Naomi swallowed hard and continued. Ruth recognized that she was choking back her tears. "I have not been the example that you women needed during your time of grief. I have been so consumed by my own that I have not done well in helping you to accept what has happened. My apology, however, stems beyond that. Before my family came to Moab the two of you were content and happy with your lot in life. You each had your own family before becoming a part of ours and, no doubt, would have married men from your own land. However, when we arrived, you took my boys as your husbands. You both became a welcome addition to our family, and though I am thankful for that, I am sorry that we came into your world, took you from the homes of your fathers and that now, you have no hope and no future." Her voice broke and a sob caught in her throat.

"Naomi, please," Ruth begged, but stopped again quickly as her mother-in-law held up her hand demanding silence. Orpah shifted uncomfortably in her place across from them and then rose to offer Naomi a strip of cloth for her tears, the first sign of compassion she had demonstrated in weeks. Naomi wiped her face, cleared her throat and began again.

"I say all that to say that thankfully, though relationships between you and your parents may be a bit strained due to your marriage to Israeli men, the two of you do have homes to which you can return. That being the case, my wish is for each of you to return to the home of your fathers. Your parents will, without a doubt, welcome you back under the current circumstances, and I am sure they will provide for you there."

"Return home?" Orpah spoke up. "You wish for us to return to our family?" Orpah cast a confused look at Ruth, tears brimming in her eyes.

"Naomi, you are our family," Ruth spoke with surety. She knew that she was speaking for both Orpah and herself. "What would become of you if we were to leave you?" she questioned honestly.

Naomi squared her shoulders and spoke with certainty. "I, myself, am going home," she promised them both. "I am older now, but I am empty here, here in this desolate land where God has taken everything from me. Therefore, I am returning to Bethlehem. I am going back to my people, and I am going back to my God. He has taken everything I have here in Moab, but perhaps He will look kindly on me once again if I return to Bethlehem, and I can at least die in peace in my homeland," Naomi rose indicating the conversation was over.

Ruth and Orpah sat in the silence and looked first at one another and then to Naomi. It was Ruth who spoke first as she stood.

"Then you will not go alone," she stated firmly. "I will go as well."

"As will I," Orpah spoke as she too rose to her feet. Ruth hid the surprise she felt from showing on her face. She was not sure if Orpah would agree to accompany them or not.

Naomi looked from one to the other and decided that their minds were made up. There would be no use to argue, especially with Ruth, and tonight, she did not have the strength to even try. "Very well," Naomi agreed, and Ruth detected a sense of relief in her voice.

"When do we leave?" Though she had no idea, Ruth had struck a blow straight to the heart of Naomi with those four words. The four words, which haunted the older woman day and night, had now been cast back at her by her unknowing daughter-in-law. Naomi prayed she was not making another mistake in allowing the women to accompany her back to Bethlehem.

Oh well, what more can be done to me, she thought to herself.

"We will gather provisions tomorrow and begin our journey the following day," she spoke quickly. "I plan to take nothing except what we will need on the journey. Besides the two of you, there is nothing I wish to remember of Moab," Naomi finished.

"So be it," Ruth acknowledged.

Naomi spoke not another word but turned and retired to the room she and Elimelech had once shared. Pulling her chair to the window that overlooked his grave, she sat in the darkness thinking once more of who she was leaving behind. The moon cast an eerie shadow over the place her husband lay.

She had come to Moab full, but in two short days she would begin the journey home to Bethlehem empty. She had come to Moab with hope and would be returning to Bethlehem hopeless. She had come to Moab with two sons and would now return to Bethlehem with two daughters, and two reminders, of all she sought to leave behind. She had been afraid when she first began her journey here, but at that time she had her husband to guide her. Now she was the guide home, and Elimelech's body would remain beneath the dirt in this foreign land alongside her two sons. This foreign soil which they were only to visit for a little while, would forever remain their final destination.

Not knowing what else to do, and not even sure she would be physically or mentally capable of completing the journey she was about to embark on, Naomi did as she was accustomed to doing. She did what felt familiar to her, and what she had done for countless hours since the day Elimelech died. She buried her face in her hands and wept.

Chapter Five

Ruth could not describe her feelings the next morning if she tried. She lay on her cot as the sun broke the morning sky, thinking of what she had agreed to the night before. She had heard Naomi sobbing as she drifted off to sleep, but that was not at all unfamiliar. Her own pillow was wet with tears most nights, but last night a different feeling had overtaken her. She pondered on this feeling in the quietness of the moment.

Leaving Moab would mean leaving all of her familiarities behind. Her biological family, the few people she still considered friends in town, the gods of her people, though she no longer worshiped them, and the sights and smells she had experienced every single day of her life. It also meant she would be leaving behind the grave which held her husband, the grave that she visited every day, the location where their wedding ceremony was held which she passed each time she went into town, and the well where she had first met Mahlon. She would leave behind the home he had held her in, the home that was once filled with promise and the hope of a future together, and she would leave behind the mountain view. She turned to look out her window. Those very mountains she saw each time she looked out, which used to be one her favorite sights, now held a bitter reminder of where his body had been found broken and cold. Yes, though there were many things she would miss by leaving Moab, there were also many things she was ready to escape from.

She rose as the sun's rays broke through her window and pulled a shawl about her shoulders, silently stepping through the house and then out the door avoiding waking her mother and sister-in-law. This feeling she was experiencing was bittersweet. She almost smiled as she gathered small sticks to start a fire and began to prepare not only their morning meal, but also provisions for their journey. A quiet excitement had crept into her heart. Excitement to leave behind this sadness and the pagan gods that would always be rooted in Moab, and excitement to find out more about the God she now served in the land that was His and the land of her late husband's. Surely if Bethlehem was all Naomi had described it as before the famine came, and if God was blessing the people there again as her friend had described, He would bless them upon their arrival there. Ruth did not know what her future held, but she knew Who held her future.

By the time Naomi and Orpah emerged from their rooms, Ruth had a second cake of bread on the coals and hot porridge boiling in the kettle.

"Good morning," she smiled softly as they took their place at the table. Setting a bowl of porridge in front of each of them, Ruth wasted no time jumping right into a conversation. "I took the liberty of beginning to prepare provisions for our journey. Is there anything special you feel we will need, Naomi?" Ruth took a seat with them as they ate. As usual, Orpah barely picked at the food in front of her but taking a cue from Ruth, she too attempted to encourage her mother-in-law.

"What can I do to help prepare?" Orpah asked quietly.

Naomi sat in silence studying the women before her. When she finally spoke, it was direct and matter of fact.

"We will not be able to take anything other than what we can carry in our arms or on our backs, mostly only food and water. When my family traveled to Moab, we were able to complete the journey in only seven days. I fear the trip back may take a bit longer, but we should still be able to make our way in nine to ten days at most."

"But Bethlehem is just across the river," Orpah spoke up. "Will it really take that long?"

Naomi spoke softly to her daughter-in-law, not surprised that it was Orpah who had voiced the question.

"Yes, it is," she agreed, "but unless you are prepared for a great swim across the Dead Sea, we must go around the river, not across it," she explained kindly, a small smile lifting her lips. Orpah realized the jest for what it was, clearly surprised that her mother-in-law was teasing her. Smiling softly, she simply nodded in understanding. Naomi continued. "We should be able to make it to the Arnon River on day one. We can make camp along this side of the riverbank and rest there on our first night. Though the rains have been few lately, and the river should be shallow enough that we can cross it easily, I would prefer to be well rested before we make the crossing." She looked to her daughters-in-law for their thoughts. When neither of them had any objection to her plan, she continued. "After we cross the Arnon, we will continue across the plains of Moab. That should take us two, maybe three days before we arrive at our next crossing, the Jordan River."

"I have heard of the Jordan River in a story told by my people when we were children," Ruth spoke up, "and Mahlon spoke of it once."

"That was much more than a story, my dear," Naomi explained. "That is history, the history of our people. You will see remnants of the walls of Jericho as soon as the river is crossed."

"The great city, where the walls fell," Orpah questioned, "are those stories true?"

"Very much," Naomi affirmed, "but that is a story for another time. It is after we cross the

Jordan River and continue along the outskirts of what was Jericho that we will begin our ascent into Bethlehem. That will be our most difficult task, but once we complete it, we will be at the end of our journey. A day to cross the Jordan, and two or three more days to make the ascent up the mountain, and we will be home."

Naomi stopped and looked at her daughters. It made her tired just to think of it, but her mind was made up. She saw the concern on the other women's faces.

"I realize that I am much older now than I was when I first made such a journey, but I am determined to do this. I appreciate the willingness of each of you to accompany me, but now that you have heard how difficult this journey may be, I completely understand if either, or both of you have changed your mind and wish to remain here, in Moab."

"My mind has not changed," Ruth spoke quickly. "If you are determined to make this journey, then I am determined to go with you." Naomi sensed that determination in Ruth's voice.

Orpah appeared to be lost in thought. "I did not realize the journey would be so long," she finally spoke honestly, "and I have never ventured beyond our borders and was not aware of the landscapes we would have to cross, but I, too, will go." Ruth noticed the hesitancy in Orpah's voice but hoped it was only her nerves that made her appear hesitant. Truthfully, she herself was fearful of the unknown, of the obstacles they may encounter on their trip that their mother-in-law had not anticipated, but more than her fear of the crossing was her fear of Naomi making the crossing alone.

Their plan in place, the women spent the rest of their day preparing for their journey. Ruth and Naomi filled leather jugs with water and grain, continued to bake and wrap cakes of bread, then packed, and repacked sacks, knowing their load would be limited to their individual abilities. Orpah worked on her own supplies, but spent most of her day outside alongside the grave of her former husband, Chilion.

"Tomorrow cannot come quickly enough," she heard Naomi utter as she watched Orpah at the grave. "I am more than ready to put Moab behind me."

Ruth placed a hand on her arm. "As am I," she spoke honestly. "Though I am not quite sure that Orpah feels as confident about it as we do."

"Are you certain, Ruth?" Naomi questioned her again. "Are you sure that you want to leave your home and go into a completely foreign land? There are no promises there," she spoke honestly.

"I am certain." Ruth assured her plainly. "I am certain that the promises of God rest in that place, and I am certain that in His land is where I, too, long to be."

By the time the sun was low in the sky everything they could possibly carry was placed by the door. They had settled on a few small sacks of meal for porridge, a small cruse of oil and several cakes of bread wrapped tightly together and bundled so as not to spoil. Another sack contained one pot for cooking and a cup for each of them to drink from, along with several leather jugs of water. Finally, in a smaller satchel, Ruth had stuffed one extra robe for each of them and a small blanket each for Naomi and Orpah. Ruth had commissioned her own blanket as a satchel to carry their goods. She was certain she could keep herself warm by the fire each night, and though not ideal, she would make do.

As she lay down, she realized that for the first night in more than she could count, Naomi's quiet sobs did not lull her to sleep. Actually, she believed the older woman had fallen asleep much faster than normal. It could be as simple as the fact that her day had been filled with something other than her grieving. She had worked hard alongside Ruth packing, preparing, and baking, and that was something she had not done as of late. Or it could be that she was so looking forward to going home, her grief had failed to consume her this night. Regardless as to why, Ruth was just beginning to doze into her own peaceful, and much needed sleep, when she heard Orpah softly call to her.

"Ruth," Orpah whispered as she touched her arm. "Are you sleeping?"

Ruth sat up quickly, struggling to keep the sleep from her voice. "I, I am not," she spoke truthfully, jolting wide-awake as she perched on the side of her cot. "Is something wrong?" she asked.

"Are you frightened?" Orpah asked, and Ruth caught the tremor in her voice. "Are you sure about traveling so far away?" Orpah sat down on the edge of the cot alongside Ruth.

"I would be lying if I said I was not nervous about the journey," Ruth spoke quietly. "But I truly believe it is what is needed. I feel if Naomi returns to her people and to her home that God will help to heal and lessen her grief over time."

"My grief will never go away," Orpah spoke truthfully. Her voice remained a whisper but was firm.

"But time will heal, and God will heal," Ruth spoke honestly. "I miss Mahlon every single day, Orpah, but as he taught me, God has a reason and a purpose for everything. I want to go to Bethlehem to help Naomi and to help myself grow closer to the God this family serves and Who they have taught me to serve."

"But if what they have said is true, their people may not accept us there," Orpah argued. "Chilion told me that their God had warned them against even coming to Moab, much less joining in with us. As Moabite people, we will be shunned and ignored. At least here in Moab we would be accepted and loved as we are. In time, they would forget we had ever married Israelites."

"If the people in Bethlehem serve God as they should, they will recognize that we are there to do the same. It may take some time, but I believe given time, they will show us mercy as

He has shown them in ending their famine and in bringing Naomi back to her home. Elimelech's family was well-loved in Bethlehem, and I am sure the people there have missed them terribly."

"But THEY are not returning!" Orpah spoke harshly, her voice a bit loud. She caught herself as Naomi stirred, though she did not wake. She lowered her voice before speaking again. "I admire you for your faith, Ruth, but I cannot pretend to be optimistic about a future in Bethlehem. I will go because I said I would go, but I do not have unrealistic expectations about merciful people or a merciful God. Where was His mercy when He took Elimelech from Naomi and then took our husbands from us? Naomi has always felt it was punishment for their coming to Moab to begin with. I do not see the mercy in that. I only see anger. And now she is taking Moabites back to that land with her? Will her God even allow us to remain there? Will their people?" Ruth did not have an answer. In truth, though she had never allowed the thought to grow, she had wondered the same thing. But now was not the time to admit that to Orpah. "I hope I am wrong," Orpah continued as she stood, "but I am afraid of what we are agreeing to."

Orpah turned and moved back to her own cot. Ruth watched as she settled down, and then laid down herself once again. Her mind wandered back and forth now between the good times she had with Mahlon and the sadness she had felt because of losing him. She contemplated on all Orpah had said and questioned her own reasoning. She would admit that she was still learning about the God of the Israelites, but she knew how to pray to Him, which she did before falling into a fitful sleep. She prayed that by going to Bethlehem with Naomi she was doing as she should. She prayed for strength for them all in the journey to come. And then she prayed, as earnestly and as humbly as she knew how, for God to have mercy upon her for being a Moabite.

Chapter Six

Ruth woke suddenly but lay completely still wondering what had awoken her. She was certain she had heard a noise, but now she heard nothing now as she lay in the silence. She pushed herself up enough that she could see the cot where Orpah lay still curled in her usual fetal position finally sleeping soundly after a restless night. Ruth sat up far enough to look out the window where a movement in the distance caught her eye. Quietly, she moved closer to get a better view.

In the early morning light, she could just make out a figure now seated at the graves of the three most important men in her world. It was Naomi. *She is finally saying her goodbyes,* Ruth thought to herself. Her first instinct was to go to her mother-in-law, to hold her as she cried and to grieve with her one final time, but instead, she opted to give the woman her space. Ruth herself had taken some time just before nightfall the night before and gone to that exact same spot for one last time. She had lain across the grave of Mahlon, sobbing until her tears were spent, before vowing never to return there again. God had allowed her the privilege of being joined to Mahlon, brought her to Himself through their union, and then taken her husband from her. She still had no understanding of it all, but she had acceptance. She prayed Naomi was finally finding the same acceptance of that fact as well.

Ruth rose and busied herself, quickly dressing before making a few last-minute preparations for their journey. They would break the fast here before beginning their trip, and in truth, Ruth was more than ready to go. Just as she was setting hot porridge on the table, Naomi returned. Her face was streaked with tears, but her eyes told Ruth she was ready to go and to let go. Orpah had finally stirred and was at the table as well, as the ladies quickly and quietly consumed the food before them.

Just moments later, loads in their arms and packs across their backs, Ruth pulled the door closed behind them and turned to face her fellow travelers.

"You are certain you are ready for this journey?" Naomi questioned them once more. The load of goods she bore was much lighter than Ruth's but not as light as Orpah's.

"I am ready," Ruth spoke with surety.

Oprah nodded her head affirming she was as ready as she was going to be, and their journey began. Banter was light as they began to travel, each shifting goods here and there to make their loads more bearable. The possessions they left behind had been sold to a local who was more than willing to take what few things they had off their hands. He had, however, required their one donkey as well, which Ruth had obliged, thinking it would be one less mouth to feed as they traveled. She questioned her thinking on that as they moved along now, wondering if maybe she should have pressed the issue and insisted on keeping the beast.

They continued in silence for the majority of the morning, and as the sun continued to move across the sky, Ruth could see that Naomi was beginning to grow tired. They had not traveled enough to call it a day, but she felt a rest was necessary if they wanted to continue until nightfall. Ruth, being at the front of the small party, paused at the base of a tall Juniper tree allowing some of her baggage to fall from her shoulder. Fortunately, the heat of the day was not unbearable, but the shade the tree offered would be nice.

"I believe a rest is in order," she suggested to her companions. "And I am about to perish for a drop of water," she admitted with a smile. She lowered the largest of the packs from her back as Naomi took refuge under the shade of the tree, settling against one of the larger roots to rest her legs.

"I have never been this far from the village, nor did I ever plan to be," Orpha complained as she dropped her packs to the ground. Ruth handed her the water jug she had just drunk from. Orpah accepted it and took a long drink. "How many days of this must we endure?" she asked as she wiped the sweat from the back of her neck. Naomi was quiet, but Ruth recognized uneasiness in her features. She was about to question her well-being when Naomi spoke.

"It is not too late," the older woman said finally. "Our journey has barely begun. You may still return to your homes. In fact, you should," she stated plainly. "Go home, to your parents. The Lord will deal kindly with you, as ye have dealt with the dead and with me. He will give each of you rest, and you still have time to find husbands." Ruth looked to Naomi as if she had taken leave of her senses. Orpah looked at her with tears in her eyes.

"Naomi, we have been through this," Ruth spoke, offering her a crust of bread. "You are tired and hungry. We will rest here for a bit, and then we will all feel like continuing our journey." Ignoring the bread she offered, Naomi grabbed Ruth, pulling her into a fierce embrace, kissing her cheek as she released her.

"You have been so good to me," she sobbed now, "and I will be forever grateful for your kindness. Kindness shown by both of you," she added, looking to Orpah and extending her hand. "But there is no good reason for you to continue this journey with me. You are tired and worn, and we have only been walking a few hours. And why should you continue with me? Are there more sons in my womb of which you could marry? I am too old to have a husband, yet if I should say that I have hope, and would have a husband tonight, would you tarry for my sons until they are grown?" Ruth recognized the heavy grief in Naomi's voice and allowed her to continue speaking, though she realized she really should be saving the strength she was exerting for their journey. Even so, Ruth could not escape her own tears which trailed her face at the realization of Naomi's words. "It grieveth me for your sakes that the hand of the Lord has gone out against me. Please, go back to your people and go back to your gods. Return to your homeland as I return to mine. Go and find husbands and a future for yourself, for I can offer you none."

Naomi buried her face in her hands and wept; the excitement of the past days, the finality of the graves she was leaving behind, and the uncertainty as to what she was returning to, all taking its toll on her emotions. Ruth was surprised when Orpah stepped in front of Naomi, took her face in her hands, and placed a simple kiss on her withered cheek. Quickly, she turned to Ruth, who was standing by wiping her own tears in silence.

"I am sorry," Orpah spoke truthfully, and Ruth knew she honestly meant it though she could not believe what was about to happen. "I cannot do this," Orpah finished bridging the gap between them and hugging her sister-in-law tightly. The embrace lasted for only a moment before Orpah pulled away, picked up the one bag that contained only her belongings, and began to quickly walk away from them, beginning her personal journey back to Moab. Ruth watched her go in silence, noticing that Orpah's steps were much faster now that she was headed in the opposite direction and that she never looked back to the women she was quickly leaving behind.

"Ruth," Naomi spoke, breaking the silence and wiping her tears, "go. Behold, your sister-in-law has gone back unto her people and unto her gods; return with her."

Ruth shook her head in denial. "I will not," she spoke fiercely as she ran to her mother-in-law. For the first time in weeks, she allowed Naomi to see her suffering. "Stop asking me to leave you," she cried, as she held tightly to the one person she cared most about in the world. Her own tears began in a torrent now, and she was not ashamed of them. "Whither thou goest, I will go; and where thou lodgest, I will lodge: thy people shall be my people, and thy God my God: Where thou diest, will I die, and there will I be buried: the Lord do so to me, and more also, if ought but death part thee and me." Ruth sobbed openly wetting Naomi's tunic with her tears. "Please, Naomi. Please, stop asking me to return from you," she begged.

Naomi realized at that moment how determined Ruth was. She was also ashamed of herself for her constant insistence that had broken this woman, this woman who had seemed unbreakable, by pressing her repeatedly to leave her and return to her own people. It finally occurred to Naomi, not only how important Ruth was to her, but also how important she was to Ruth.

Ruth had been a constant reminder to Naomi of all she had lost, but Naomi was a reminder to Ruth of all she had gained. Ruth had gained love as she had never imagined from Naomi's family and the truth about a God who would never forsake or leave her. Naomi wept over her own selfishness and vowed silently that she would never again ask Ruth to leave her side. When Ruth's sobbing finally subsided and she raised her head, Naomi brushed the hair from her face.

"Very well," she concluded simply, one more tear spilling onto her own withered cheek. "We shall continue our journey together," she said as she stood. Ruth straightened herself and wiped her face with her own tunic, then turned to collect the baggage. There was more to carry since Orpah had gone, but Ruth did not want Naomi to accumulate the load Orpah had left behind. Shifting items here and there allowed her to carry the extra things.

The two women continued on, though their emotions had utterly drained their energy, and by evening they had reached the Arnon River just as Naomi had predicted when they had planned their journey. Though the water did look low enough to allow them a fairly easy passage across, Ruth decided to stick to Naomi's original plan and camp on this side of the river tonight. She wanted her mother-in-law well rested and sure footed when they forged even the shallow water.

The two ladies made their camp, Naomi pulling blankets and wraps from their packs as Ruth worked to build a simple fire. They dined on the dried meat Ruth had packed and hot bowls of porridge cooked over the fire.

"Tell me of Jericho," Ruth began. "You said there was a story there for a later time. I think we have time now," she grinned as she stoked the fire. Naomi watched as the flames danced, a small smile playing on her lips.

"I do not know all you have been taught of our people, Ruth," she began. "But we have always been of the stubborn kind," she admitted honestly. "After the Israelites were freed from slavery in Egypt, Moses led them through the wilderness in search of the land God had promised them, their Promised Land, a land flowing with milk and honey. For forty years they wandered, being fed only by God with manna from the Heavens, being led by a cloud by day and a pillar of fire by night."

"Forty years? And we fret over a ten-day journey!" Ruth admitted. "Forty years is an awfully long time to wander. Surely, they could have settled somewhere," Ruth spoke truthfully.

"It was not to be," Naomi clarified. "They were told they would be given the Promised Land and some of them doubted. They did not trust God, as they should have, to help them take what was rightfully theirs, even though it had been established by the enemy. Because of their disbelief, they were cursed to wander, and wander they did until Joshua arose and became the leader God expected him to be. The leader who led them into the land God had promised them."

"How did he do it?" Ruth asked simply. She had heard parts of the story as a child, but she had never heard Naomi's version, and she was strangely curious. Ruth stretched her legs before the fire, clearly intent on learning all she could.

"Joshua stood with his company on the brinks of the Jordan River. Jericho was well fortified, and upon first glance, he knew there was no way he could penetrate the walls of that great city alone," Naomi continued. "He sent spies into the city, and when they returned to him, they verified all he had expected. It would take God alone to conquer those walls."

"What did he do?" Ruth asked, clearly enchanted by all she was hearing.

"Joshua was instructed by a Captain of the Lord's Host as to how to defeat Jericho. The angel gave him specific instructions that the Israelites were to march around the city once every day for six days. On the seventh day, they were to march seven times around and after their seventh march, they were to sound their trumpets and give a shout. They did exactly as they were instructed, and when the people shouted, the walls fell! Our people were able to ascend upon the people of Jericho and defeat them, laying claim on the land and destroying the sinful city it had become."

"So, the ruins of the city are still there?" Ruth asked curiously.

"They are. And you shall see them once we cross the Jordan River," Naomi smiled at her.

"Our God is so powerful," Ruth admitted. "How could anyone ever doubt Him?" she wondered aloud.

"Because, so often, our faith waivers due to our lack of ability to see with our eyes. It is then that we must see with our heart, trusting in what we know is there." Naomi spoke aloud but Ruth realized Naomi herself was taking in her own words. "We must have faith, believing in the things we cannot see," she finished.

"You are tired, Naomi," Ruth spoke frankly, "as am I. Let us rest so that we can continue our journey early tomorrow before the heat of the day." Naomi nodded in agreement and before Ruth could clear away the remnants of their meal, the older woman was sound asleep.

Chapter Seven

Day two of their journey dawned bright and clear, and it did not take long for the women to break their fast and continue on their way. Their crossing of the Arnon River was uneventful, and laughter even ensued as the women dipped their feet into the cool water which eventually barely reached their knees. Though the water was low and moving very slowly, Ruth kept a careful watch on Naomi as they crossed and thanked God above when they had made their way safely to the other side.

On they walked, and the day passed quickly. They had passed no one since they had left the borders of Moab, and Ruth was glad for the seclusion. Time and again throughout the day, she realized that with each step she took, she was farther away from the things she had always known and closer to all the things she had yet to know. Realizing their solitude, thoughts began to creep into her mind of robbers and thieves, bandits, and stray animals. After all, they were two women alone in the plains of Moab; what an easy target they would be! Each time a thought of those things tried to form, Ruth would whisper a silent prayer to God for protection and peace as she attempted to lead Naomi back to her home and back to Him.

"We made good time today," Naomi stated when they stopped again for the night. "I dare say one more day of crossing this desert and we shall be upon the banks of the Jordan River.

"Should we take an extra day to rest then?" Ruth asked sincerely. "I know you are eager, but I also remember you stating the hardest part of our journey waits across the river."

"We shall see how we fare," Naomi spoke with thought. "The ascent into Bethlehem will be far more treacherous than when we descended years ago, and I admit that I can feel my years in these old legs," she laughed.

Ruth moved to the feet of her mother-in-law and began to remove her dusty sandals. Naomi attempted to move her feet away, but Ruth held fast to her foot. "No, Naomi, I insist," she spoke plainly looking into the old woman's eyes.

Naomi relinquished and allowed Ruth to pour water from their supply over her tired feet and to wash them with her tunic. Ruth's own feet ached, but she recognized the blisters that were forming on Naomi's and quickly fetched some ointment she had tucked away discreetly.

"Where did you get that?" Naomi asked as Ruth gently massaged the ointment onto the sores that were beginning to form. Ruth smiled at her mother-in-law. "I have not given away all of my secrets," she laughed. "When I was a child, my grandmother taught me ways to create medicines from the roots around our small village. I do not believe in the healing powers she taught me of; I know that Jehovah God alone holds the power to heal, but I do know that this ointment can ease some of the pain we feel from those physical ailments. It was He who created the roots, after all."

Naomi allowed her to continue, wondering how she had never known of this until now, and she then realized how little Ruth had spoken of her years as a child.

"Tell me more of your childhood," she insisted, and Ruth did. She shared stories of life in Moab as she grew, both good and bad and Naomi knew when she finished just how destitute and desolate life had been for Ruth before meeting Mahlon and his family. Why in the world would Orpah want to return to such a land? And Naomi could not help but wonder once again why Elimelech would have ever thought it a good idea to go there.

However, the past was in the past and Naomi was determined to only look forward. Besides, God had brought them a blessing even in their sinful state by allowing Ruth to become a part of their family. Where would Naomi be without her now?

As Ruth began to sleep softly, try as she might, Naomi could not stop the constant thought that plagued her mind. How would her people in Bethlehem react to her Moabitess daughter-in-law? She would know for certain within the next week, and besides, it did not matter. Never again would she try to push Ruth away.

The next day passed quickly and the ladies made good time once again. Ruth's steps were sure and steady though she could tell Naomi was growing tired. Even so, just as Naomi suspected, they reached the banks of the Jordan River right before nightfall. Ruth prepared camp while Naomi once again took shelter under a lonely tree which had somehow managed to sprout and grow in the dusty plain.

Ruth stood on the bank and took in the expanse of the river before her. In the distance, she could see the remains of the wall of Jericho and thought of the story Naomi had so recently shared with her. Even with only remnants of the wall still standing, Ruth could make out how majestic they must have been, and what an obstacle they must have presented to Joshua and company. She could not help but notice one wall, continuing to stand tall and tower above the others. A single window near the top winked at her. *How interesting that that wall remains,* she thought to herself.

A glance back at Naomi allowed Ruth to observe her resting comfortably. Ruth allowed herself a moment to petition Jehovah.

"Dear Lord," she prayed softly as she sank to her knees, "I am asking you for your provisions. I know Naomi is tired and she is worn, as am I, dear Father. God, I humbly ask that you grant us safety as we cross this river tomorrow. Lord, I do not know how deep this river is before us, but You do. I do not know how to assure safe passage for Naomi and myself, but I know that You do. I do not know what lies beyond the banks of this river in the mountains that lie just on the other side, but You do. Help me Father, to do Your will in all that is to come. Show me, as you showed Joshua when he stood on the bank of this very river and saw the vast walls of Jericho before him, how I am to proceed. I need your guiding hand and your protection just as he did, dear Lord. Help me to be obedient, and help me to be and to do all that you ask of me."

"Amen," Naomi sounded right behind her. Ruth jumped and stood with her hand over her heart.

"Naomi! For a moment I thought you were an angel from God that had come in an answer to my prayer!"

Naomi looked into the face of the young woman before her. "Ruth, you have done so much for me, and again, I find myself in awe of the strength you possess for one so new to our faith. You have done an amazing job on our journey so far, and God will reward you for your strength. He will not fail us now."

Ruth hugged her mother-in-law and looked across the river. "So those are the walls of Jericho," she stated as she looked again at the mass of stone and rubble.

"The land of giants," Naomi answered as she herself took in the vast amount of debris that seemed to be scattered for miles. "I'm so glad to know that our God is mightier than those walls," she smiled to Ruth.

The ladies turned to make their way back toward the place they would camp for the night. Ruth seemed to step a little lighter, and Naomi wished her faith was as confident in her heart as it was in the words she had just spoken to Ruth.

Once they had finished their meager meal and Ruth had put away what was left of their provisions, the women sat quietly around their small fire. Though the days were warm, the nights were cool and the warmth the small flame put out was a welcome one. The moon was bright this night and though Naomi had spoken with confidence earlier, Ruth noticed a restlessness in her as they sat.

"Are you anxious about returning home, Naomi?" Ruth asked softly.

"Yes, and no," Naomi answered truthfully as she stared into the flames. "I am looking forward to being home in Bethlehem; I am just not sure what will be left of my memories once we arrive there. I know some of our friends and loved ones are bound to have passed on either due to age or perhaps the famine which drove us from our land, and I wonder as to the state of the home we left. Has someone else laid claim to it, or does it even still stand? But above all," she continued as tears filled her eyes, "I can barely imagine being back there without

Elimelech and my boys. They are, after all, what made our dwelling the home that it was."

Ruth allowed Naomi the solitude she seemed to crave. She didn't speak or ask for more clarification, and she didn't try to fill the silence with a declaration that she was her family now because Ruth knew she nor anyone else could ever fill the void Naomi felt in losing her husband and her sons. She just listened as Naomi began to softly recount stories of their lives before the famine.

She spoke of how she met Elimelech and how they came to build their life together. She spoke of the joy they had felt when she had given Elimelech not one but two sons. She spoke of old friendships they had shared and how those friendships became strained once the famine began. As the night waned, her voice grew softer until, at last, she settled down and slept.

Ruth never once said a word but moved only to pull a blanket to cover Naomi's frail shoulders before she laid down herself. Her sleep did not come easy but did come eventually as she repeated her earlier prayer time and again softly to herself and to God alone.

Lord, please help me get her safely home.

Chapter Eight

The activity of the previous days took a toll the next morning, and though both ladies slept well, neither of them stirred with the sunrise as they had previous mornings. It was still early when Ruth began to hear a man's voice issuing commands nearby. She could tell the voice was not directed to anyone in their camp but sounded as if it were coming from the river. Confused and still dazed, she rose to see what the fuss was about.

"Yah! Yah!" the man yelled, "Move you filthy beast!" Ruth rose and rubbed her eyes as she stumbled to the edge of the river to get a better view of the commotion. Lodged just off the banks was a wagon loaded with goods. A portly gentleman was at the reins, lashing at a poor donkey who was clearly struggling. They had not made it very far across, the water only covering the bottom portion of the wagon wheel, but the animal was unable to pull the wagon forward, or to move it backward. What the man could not see, but Ruth was just able to make out, was that it was the wagon wheel which was refusing to move, not the animal. It appeared that just beneath the surface of the water a large stone or some other obstacle was preventing the wheel from turning forward.

The man continued to issue his commands, urging the beast to move, but because his back was to her, Ruth had a hard time getting his attention. She moved up and down the riverbank, attempting to gain an audience with him.

"Sir!" she yelled, "Excuse me! Sir," she continued as she waved her arms from the shore line. Her pleas were to no avail since his commands to his donkey were so close together. Ruth was shocked to the core when Naomi moved up beside her with a small stone in her hand. One quick motion, and the rock smacked the man right in his back. Quickly, he turned around in his seat and noticed the women, Ruth staring wide-eyed in disbelief at her mother-in-law for what she had done.

"Pardon me, ladies," the man yelled from his seat in the wagon. "I did not mean to disturb you!" he apologized. "For whatever reason, my donkey has lost all strength and refuses to budge another inch! I must get these goods to Bethlehem; I cannot afford to lose them all in the river!"

Ruth snapped from her trance. "Sir!" she responded, directing her attention from Naomi to him once again. "Your wagon cannot move because your wheel is lodged!" she called to him.

"What say ye?" he responded turning more in his seat to better see her.

"Your wagon wheel! It is lodged in the water!" she yelled louder placing her hands on each side of her lips to direct her voice.

"I cannot hear you!" he responded beginning to grow agitated at being bothered by these women.

"YOUR. WAGON. IS. STUCK!" Naomi yelled at a capacity Ruth would never have imagined her capable of.

"Well why in the world did you not tell me sooner!" he yelled back getting off the wagon seat and lowering himself into the water. It came almost to his knees. The water was moving much faster than the Arnon had been, which had been almost still at their crossing. This river seemed to have had rain recently as it rushed violently around the man's legs. Ruth noticed he seemed to be somewhat struggling himself, and he was not nearly as small in stature as herself and Naomi.

Ruth had no doubt she could make it to the point where the man was, but deeper into the river the danger was certain to grow more treacherous. How would she ever get herself and Naomi across?

Ruth watched as he approached his back wagon wheel and reached beneath the water to feel around it trying to gauge the size of his problem.

"Seems to be a rock," he yelled at them. "Problem is, I cannot budge this rock alone and guide my animal. I hate to ask, but could I impose upon the two of you ladies for some assistance. I would sincerely appreciate it."

Ruth noticed Naomi squint toward the man and at once, her face began to soften. "I know that voice," she said quietly, "Jedidiah?" she asked much louder as a smile began to crease her face.

The man stopped and looked back to the riverbank. Quickly he began making strides through the river, seemingly unworried about the current. As he approached, Naomi moved toward the water herself, and Ruth did not know if she should stop her or let her go.

"Naomi!" he exclaimed taking both of her hands in his own. "Do my eyes deceive me? I cannot believe it is you! How wonderful to see you!" Ruth stood on the riverbank watching the exchange taking place before her right at the river's edge. For the third time this morning, in only a few short moments, she had been utterly surprised. "Tell me that you all are coming home! Abigail will be thrilled!" he exclaimed.

Ruth watched as the smile that had almost graced Naomi's face fell away.

"Naomi?" he questioned at the look on her face. He strained to look around the women to the campsite. "Where are Elimelech and your boys? Have they stayed behind or gone ahead?" he asked, and Ruth caught the hope in his voice.

"Only I have returned, Jedidiah," Naomi spoke as her voice trembled. She blinked rapidly and Ruth could sense Naomi was not able to voice anything further. She stepped forward.

"I am Ruth, Naomi's daughter-in-law, and from your exchange, I believe you are Jedidiah?" she spoke plainly, yet softly.

"It is a pleasure to make your acquaintance, young Ruth," he spoke nodding in her direction.

"Perhaps I can be of assistance to you in freeing your wagon from the river," she pointed, reminding him of his precious cargo still standing in the rushing water.

Jedidiah jumped to attention having completely forgotten his wares.

"I, too am able bodied enough to help," Naomi reminded them, thankful that Ruth had saved her from a dreaded conversation at just that moment.

"Absolutely not," he answered with surety. "I will not have the two of you getting yourselves soaked in the river on my account."

"Kind sir," Ruth spoke humbly. "Our plan is to forge this river to get to the other side, so getting wet will not be an option on any account."

Jedidiah looked from Ruth to Naomi and back to Ruth. "Very well, Naomi, if you could climb aboard and guide the animal, perhaps the young lady and I can free the wagon wheel."

"Very well," Ruth agreed after looking to Naomi for verification.

"Are these all your things?" he asked as he pointed to the small campsite.

"They are," Ruth affirmed.

Jedidiah moved toward them and began to roll the blankets the ladies had just vacated. "Sir, please do not feel obligated to help us. I will break our camp once we free your wagon," Ruth said quickly.

Jedidiah looked to them both. "I considered Elimelech the finest man I ever knew. I do not know what situation has brought you back to Bethlehem without him, but I will not leave his wife and her young friend stranded in the middle of the dessert. Naomi, you said you are returning to Bethlehem?" he asked for surety.

"We are," she nodded. "Ruth is my daughter-in-law, and she is returning with me."

"Then with your permission, I will escort the two of you the rest of the way. You will reach your destination a lot faster, a lot safer, and a lot easier than you would on foot."

"Accepted," Ruth spoke quickly realizing the answered prayer God had sent them. Together they quickly finished breaking camp, Jedidiah bearing most of the load that Ruth and Naomi had to bear thus far. Ruth also noticed the large branch he carried that he had retrieved from the tree that had sheltered them through the night.

He assisted Naomi as they entered the river, holding fast to her arm as the current began to wash around them. The water barely reached above her knees when they reached the wagon and Jedidiah assisted her as she hoisted up to take the reins. Ruth was not far behind them, struggling slightly but able to hold her own. As they approached the wagon wheel, Jedidiah threw all their belongings on board and instructed Ruth as to how to assist him. He would attempt to pry the wheel from the rock, and she was to push the wagon from behind.

"Be careful when throwing your weight on the wagon, so that once it is free you do not plant face first into the river," he reminded her. "Naomi, you urge the donkey forward, and once it is free, stop the animal for Ruth and I to climb aboard?"

Both ladies confirmed they understood, and their task began. Jedidiah braced the branch against the stone beginning to pry it from the wheel. Ruth pushed from behind and Naomi was at the reigns urging the animal forth. After only a moment, Ruth began to feel the wagon slowly inching forward and released her pressure. Jedidiah gave a mighty grunt forcing more of his strength onto the branch and the stone gave way. The wagon lurched forward, and Naomi pulled on the reigns to stop the donkey who was more than ready to head out of his watery bed.

Jedidiah gave the ladies an enthusiastic "thank you" and moved to help Ruth situate herself amongst his goods on the back of the wagon.

"Rest a while, young Ruth," he instructed. "You look positively worn out. I am sure you have had much of the burden of this journey. I will lead you safely to your destination now," he promised as he patted the back of her hand. Ruth could not help the tears that pooled in her eyes.

"Thank you, Jedidiah. You are truly an answer to prayer," she admitted.

Jedidiah nodded to her with a smile, and then moved into his position beside Naomi.

"Where on earth did you find such a fine, young woman?" he asked as he took control of the reigns.

"She was married to Mahlon, Jed," Naomi spoke frankly. "And you know without having to be told that she is a Moabitess."

"I shall not cast judgment until I know the story of where my dear friend is, Naomi. I respect you too much for that. But why not tell me all, painful as it may be, on our journey back to Bethlehem. You know as well as I that your return will be a notable event. When you arrive with a Moabitess daughter-in-law and no son nor husband to speak for you, your welcome home may be brief."

"Hear my story Jedidiah, so you may speak on my behalf," Naomi began as she recounted the story of all she had lost and all she had gained in Ruth, while in Moab.

It was not long before the lull of the conversation she could hear but words she could not make out, and the rocking of the wagon began to take their toll on Ruth. For the first time in days, she was able to stretch out without worrying of keeping the fire burning. She would be able to sleep without feeling as if she had to keep one ear open for bandits or stray animals. She was able to let her mind wander and not be constantly aware of Naomi's well-being.

So let her mind wander, she did. It was not thoughts that had not crossed her mind often, but this time she did not chase the memories away but allowed them to come. She thought of Mahlon and the smile she missed so desperately. She thought of their meetings at the well months before he finally asked her to join with him and be his wife. She thought of the place where they were married, and she thought of the grave that held him now. Ruth was worn and her emotions overcame her. The journey, caring for Naomi, her own loss, and extreme exhaustion finally took over, and though the blankets she used for pillows were soaked with her tears, she slept.

Chapter Nine

Ruth did not know how long she slept before the increased jostling of the wagon woke her. She could tell they were climbing a mountain and was increasingly thankful they were doing so in a wagon and not on foot. She raised up to get a better view of her surroundings and was not surprised when Naomi noticed her movement immediately.

"It will not be much longer now," Naomi called to her. "Your prayers to Jehovah were not in vain. We will be home well before nightfall, days ahead of what it would have taken us on foot." Ruth nodded her head and smiled a small smile in Naomi's direction. She did not miss the almost reluctant tone in her voice as Naomi mentioned they would be home so quickly.

"Let us stretch our legs for a quick moment," Jedidiah spoke pulling the animal to a stop. Carefully he assisted Naomi from her place up top of the wagon, and then came around to assist Ruth from the back. Both ladies stretched their backs though their legs seemed reluctant to be back in action. The days in the dessert and crossing the rivers had taken a toll on both of their bodies.

Jedidiah pulled pieces of dried meat from a sack, and Ruth pulled what was left of the bread from hers. Sharing the fare proved to be a delightful meal for all of them.

"You ladies could use a hot meal, I am sure. Please plan to join my family for our meal tonight?" he asked them. Ruth looked to Naomi for she knew nothing of what to expect when they came to the city.

"We sincerely appreciate the invitation, Jedidiah, but I am quite eager to see what remains of the home I left behind," Naomi answered honestly.

Jedidiah nodded his understanding.

"The structure is still there, Naomi, but there will be some minor repairs to be done. Abigail and I have seen to any major upkeep, she never believed you were gone forever, but a thorough cleaning and a few nails here and there will need to be tended to."

Ruth saw Naomi visibly exhale a sigh of relief. Clearly, the condition of the structure they were returning to had weighed heavily on her mind. In Ruth's thinking, Jedidiah's clear explanation meant that no one else had laid claim on the empty structure, a thought that had plagued her mind more than once.

When Naomi continued to hesitate at accepting the invitation, Jedidiah made another offer.

"I understand your desire to get settled, Naomi. Perhaps you can join us soon, but tonight you will allow me to bring something over for the two of you," he bargained.

"That would be wonderful," Ruth agreed as she took the liberty of accepting his invitation. She had also realized, which Naomi had not, that she had taken the last of their bread from her satchel. She knew not what all, but was certain that there would be much to do when they arrived, and she would appreciate not having to prepare a meal as well.

The small party finished their break and began the end of their journey. True to Naomi's predictions, Ruth began to see signs of an approaching city within only a few hours. She noticed the fields on the outskirts of the town were filled with stalks of tall barley and rich grain. It was evident that the famine had ended, and Jehovah had once again blessed this land with the fruits of a bountiful harvest. Ruth began to see people walking amongst the stalks, no doubt checking them to ensure the harvest of their crops could begin soon.

As they began to approach more and more civilization, Jedidiah slowed the wagon to a leisurely pace to keep dust and debris from disturbing those who were walking amongst their crops. Ruth continued to observe and noticed that though the area, beliefs, and the people of

Bethlehem, were far different from those in Moab, their dress and looks were very similar. She had heard of women in other lands who sparingly covered their skin and wore jewels across their faces. She was thankful the women she observed now were as conservative as herself.

They continued another mile or so before they came to the city gates of Bethlehem. Ruth felt her heart quicken as they entered the bustling city. People began to stop in their tracks and intently watch as Jedidiah continued slowly through the streets. It was as if they were in disbelief of what they were seeing.

Suddenly, a woman about Naomi's age began to run by the side of the wagon.

"Is that you, Naomi? You have returned to us?" she called asking question after question.

Jedidiah pulled the wagon to a stop in the middle of town as people began to converge upon the wagon.

"Naomi has returned!" someone yelled.

"Look it is Naomi!" cried another.

Naomi helped herself down from the wagon seat as the woman who had caused the chaos embraced her fiercely.

"Finally, you are home!" the lady cried as she continued her embrace, tears coursing along her cheeks. "How I have longed for your return!" Jedidiah had come round to approach the two women and laid his hands softly on the eager woman's back.

"I told you Abigail would be eager to see you," he laughed, directing his comment to Naomi.

"I had come to the city expecting you today, husband, but what joy I find in that you have returned with my long lost and dearest friend," she cried.

Many took their turn in welcoming Naomi back home. Finally, she wiped her tear-filled eyes and spoke.

"Call me not Naomi, call me Mara," she instructed them, "for the Almighty hath dealt very bitterly with me," she finished as tears again streaked her face.

"Naomi, whatever has happened?" the woman called Abigail asked as Jedidiah moved to support Naomi. "Where is your family?"

"I went out full," she admitted, "and the Lord hath brought me home again empty: why then call ye me Naomi, seeing the Lord hath testified against me, and the Almighty hath afflicted me?"

It was Jedidiah who spoke when Naomi could no longer do so. He spoke plainly from her side as Abigail again wrapped Naomi in a fierce embrace.

"Naomi has returned to us, along with her daughter-in-law, Ruth. However, the bodies of Elimelech, Mahlon, and Chilion will forever remain in Moab," he finished, loud enough for the crowd to hear.

"Daughter-in-law?" a man from the crowd questioned. "Did you say her daughter-in-law?"

"She did not leave Bethlehem with a daughter-in-law," a woman spoke up from the crowd. Ruth kept her view downcast, not willing to make eye contact with anyone in the crowd.

"One of her son's took a wife in Moab?" another asked.

"Both of her sons took Moabite women for their wife, and one of those women has been kind enough to escort Naomi home to us." Jedidiah spoke plainly. "Nothing else will be said on that matter today," he finished addressing everyone in the crowd.

Ruth, who had not moved from her place on the back of the wagon, felt extremely saddened and awkward during the exchange, but what bothered her the most was that the townspeople were more worried about the Moabite among them than the fact that one of their own had returned so broken. Jedidiah assisted Naomi back to her place on the seat in the front of the wagon, Abigail squeezing in beside her.

Once seated, Abigail turned offering her hand to Ruth behind her, who had scrunched into the back of the wagon as close as space would allow. Ruth accepted her hand, and the sweet lady squeezed her hand to comfort her.

"Welcome to Bethlehem," she spoke, "and thank you for returning Naomi to us." Ruth offered a small smile in acknowledgement, thankful for at least one woman in the town, other than Naomi, who did not disregard her immediately.

"Let us get the two of you ladies home," Jedidiah spoke reigning the donkey into action. Ruth looked up when they began to move and watched the townspeople glare as the wagon pulled away. Across the crowd, she caught sight of the woman, Miriam, she had met in Moab.

Fortunately, it did not take long before the town and the people gathered there begin to disappear from view, but Ruth was certain some of them never stopped gawking in her direction until the wagon was out of sight. She knew the family who was assisting them were obviously okay with a Moabite living among them, but obviously not the rest of the town.

Ruth shook her head to dispel the negative thoughts and took in the landscape around her. Again, fields of barley rose high on either side and she could not help but be in awe of the blue sky and golden corn reaching toward the heavens. God truly had blessed this land with rich crops this year. It was positively beautiful.

As she took in the sights, she noticed a man, who appeared by his dress to be the owner of the field they were currently passing, in deep conversation with another, quite possibly the overseer of the crop. They were quite far from the road, but Ruth observed the handsome owner gently but thoroughly inspecting the ears of corn heavy on their stalks. He appeared to be very pleased with what he saw. She watched as he clasped the other man on his shoulder seemingly in praise for a job well done. The pleasant exchange brought a smile to Ruth's face as she saw the appreciation and approval being bestowed on the overseer who was clearly relieved that he was receiving such praise of the owner.

When the supposed owners gaze shifted and he met Ruth's, her face flamed at being caught watching the private exchange. Quickly she lowered her eyes ashamed with herself for staring at the strangers. A quick glance again as they continued past eased her shame however, as she noticed the owner continuing to watch her. Meeting her eyes with his own, he simply smiled and bowed his head in her direction. She allowed another small smile as they passed, noticing the kindness she saw in his eyes, then looked away determined not to turn her head that way again.

In just a few short moments another group of homes came into view. Jedidiah pulled to a stop in front of a smaller structure, but when no one made a motion to move, Ruth also kept her place assuming this was not the home she would share with Naomi. With a shrill whistle from himself a young girl, appearing a little younger than Ruth, came from the corner of the barn.

"Welcome home, Father!" she yelled as she ran toward the wagon.

Jedidiah jumped down and hugged his daughter enthusiastically. "Lydia, I want you to meet Naomi," he spoke motioning to the wagon seat.

"I remember Mrs. Naomi!" Lydia exclaimed as she climbed into the seat to embrace the older woman. "I am so glad you have returned. I know Mother is thrilled" she finished enthusiastically smiling toward her mother for acknowledgement.

"And this is her daughter-in-law, Ruth," Jedidiah continued motioning to the back of the wagon.

Lydia stepped down and around to the back where Ruth sat. "Ruth comes to us from the country of Moab," Jedidiah continued. "She will be living with Naomi, and we want to make sure she is welcome in Bethlehem," he finished.

Abigail smiled sweetly in Ruth's direction.

"Welcome to our town," she spoke cheerfully offering her hand to Ruth. "Any family of Naomi's is a welcome friend of mine."

Ruth smiled in confirmation of the olive branch that had been handed to her. She took Lydia's extended hand with all sincerity. "It is a pleasure to meet you, Lydia. Thank you for your kindness," she finished.

Pleasantries exchanged, the small party, Lydia included, continued on until they came to a larger establishment at the end of the road. Naomi sat in place and stared at the home in front of her. So many memories came flooding back. Ruth correctly assumed this was the home Naomi had been longing for. The home that had been shared by Ruth's husband, his brother, and his parents. She looked at the home and wondered what it was like when Mahlon was just a boy playing in the overgrown meadow beside the house.

Behind the house was a barn, suitable for several animals. Ruth could remember Mahlon talking about those animals as if they were friends of his family. Elimelech would argue and tell him that animals were for working, not loving, and Naomi would tell him to shush, to let the boy remember things the way he wanted to. Ruth smiled as she remembered the friendly banter as if it had taken place only yesterday.

Naomi broke her trance and finally allowed Jedidiah to assist her from the wagon, Ruth staying close behind her as they walked to the door of the home. Slowly, Naomi pushed open the door screeching with complaint for being disturbed after so long.

"Some cleaning will be in order," Naomi began, breaking the silence as she gazed across the front room.

A decent size table sat in the middle, surrounded with not four, but six chairs. An indoor cooking area was to the side of the table, where a fire could be made without having to leave the structure, and Ruth could make out more doorways that appeared to lead to other rooms. Not one, but two barrels sat in separate corners, and a small series of steps led to an upper room.

The sun was still high enough that there was light inside, though it was dim. Ruth noticed multiple oil lamps placed strategically around the room, on the hearth, on the table, on a small shelf near one of the barrels. There also appeared to be a cellar to store vegetables and even a cellar below that one, Ruth assumed for food preservation as well. It was clear that Elimelech had provided a very fine home for Naomi and his boys.

"Naomi, we are going to leave to give you and Ruth time to settle," Jedidiah spoke quietly. "Abigail and Lydia will be glad to assist with the cleaning come tomorrow, and I will help with any repairs that are needed," he promised.

"I will send Lydia later this evening with a meal for the two of you," Abigail reminded her as she hugged her dear friend.

"Thank you, both," Ruth spoke up, Naomi continuing to remain speechless as she gazed about the room.

"Thank you again, Ruth," Abigail surprised her saying, "for keeping Naomi safe and bringing her home to us." Ruth was surprised when the woman embraced her as if she too had been a long-lost friend.

Jedidiah and his family saw themselves out, and Ruth turned her attention back to her mother-in-law. She allowed her a moment's more of solitude before she crossed to the place where she stood. Once she reached her side, she remained silent until Naomi turned to her, slowly embracing the only person she had left. Ruth clung to Naomi, Naomi clung to Ruth, and both ladies released the torrent of emotions within them which had been continuing to build for days. They sank to the floor in one another's embrace, openly sobbing until they were further exhausted and tears would no longer come.

Chapter Ten

That final breakdown was all Naomi would allow herself. She had cried for months. She had allowed bitterness to rob her of years of her life. She was home in Bethlehem, and she longed for the peace and contentment she had once felt when she lived here with her family. Time had changed. People had changed. But Jehovah God had not changed.

Naomi decided that she was tired of that bitterness. While still in Moab, Naomi had sought forgiveness from Jehovah for her lack of faith and for doubting His love. She knew that in order for her prayer to have been sincere, she herself had to put forth some effort. Were you truly sorry for things you had done if you continue to do them? No, she decided. If she were truly sorry, she would have tried harder to let go of the bitterness that she felt. She would have forced herself to stop doubting in the Jehovah Who loved her so. Now that she was home Naomi was ready to attempt to do better in her thoughts and attitudes. She was ready to "get over" being bitter.

Ruth had fought. She had fought sorrow and had found a way to be at peace. Naomi knew that Ruth continued mourning her loss of Mahlon, but never had she given up as Naomi and Orpah had. Naomi thought back now to Orpah and how she had encouraged her to stay in Moab. Never, regardless of her current circumstances, should she have encouraged Orpah, or anyone else, to stay in such a God-forsaken place. She should have encouraged her to return to Bethlehem with her and Ruth. She should have done everything in her power to free Orpah from Moab and to bring her closer to the God she had never truly embraced. Another issue Naomi recognized needed forgiveness for.

Immediately upon her realization, she bowed her head and asked God to forgive her for being so foolish. She petitioned to Him that something she had said or perhaps the way she had lived before her grief and bitterness had set in, might resonate a spark in Orpah, and that reflection on those days and the faith Naomi had shared, might be all she needed to come to the all-knowing, all-loving God that her family served.

Once her prayer was done, she decided a plan of action should be put in place. Ruth had walked outside to view the meadows and barns, and Naomi joined her there. The sun was beginning to set, and it reminded Naomi of how beautiful Bethlehem could be.

"That barn is where we kept the animals," Naomi said as she joined Ruth and pointed to the large barn to the right of where they stood. "Elimelech was always good at growing things, and this meadow where you stand was once covered in vegetables and herbs. The barn there," she pointed to the left, "is where he would house his tooling and supplies to break the land and to plant it. I wonder if any of those tools are still there." Ruth took in the structures around them and marveled at the condition, though neither lady made a move toward them. There were definitely loose boards here and there, but things had held up well to have been neglected for so long, no doubt due to the occasional care of Jedidiah.

"And there is the meadow where the boys would disappear when there was work to be done," Naomi chuckled as she pointed to the hill between the structures. Ruth smiled at hearing the sound come from Naomi. Her laughter was far from as light as it used to be, but it was so much better than the sobs which had plagued Ruth's ears for the last several months.

"Those barns which held such promise are completely empty now," Naomi continued, "as are the meadows, the barrels of meal and oil, and the cupboards," she added with a quick glance at Ruth.

"Jehovah is already providing for our needs this evening," Ruth reminded her. "Abigail promised to send a meal for us. I will go into town tomorrow to see if I can find some things to get us through with the little money we have from the sale of our things back in Moab. That should sustain us until we find a way to provide for ourselves," she finished.

Naomi nodded her head. "Jedidiah is a wonderful man with a wonderful family. There was a time when they had nothing, and Elimelech always made sure they had food. He has not forgotten that, and though they seem to have made a way for themselves and are doing better, they still do not have a lot to give. Yet, they are willing to share what they have with us, and for that I am thankful."

As if knowing they were being talked about, Ruth heard a friendly salutation from behind them.

"Hello again!" she heard Lydia yell from the front of their home.

"We are in the back," Naomi returned.

In only a moment, Ruth saw the happy face round the corner, a basket full of provisions in her arms. Lydia had such a pretty disposition, and her physical appearance was pleasant as well, with long dark hair framing her thin face. Ruth was thankful that her attitude on the inside matched her physical appearance on the outside. Many women in Moab who were fair to look upon, were cruel and used their looks for unethical, personal gain. Their excuse for their actions were that by doing so, they were winning the favor of their god, Chemosh.

"Mother has sent enough provisions for tonight, and for tomorrow morning as well!"

Lydia spoke enthusiastically. "She has included some meal, oil, dried meats, and bread."

Ruth took the basket extended to her. "We cannot thank you enough for your kindness," she said returning the smile she was also offered.

"Tell your mother we will repay her for her generosity as soon as we are able," Naomi promised.

Lydia waved the promise away with the flick of her wrist. "You owe us nothing," she argued kindly. "The two of you returning from Moab is more than ample payment."

Ruth could not help but smile again at the young woman's enthusiasm. Her cheerful disposition was contagious.

"I will take these things inside. Ruth, visit with Lydia, she will be good company for you. You have had no one, save one old lady, to talk to lately," Naomi winked as she walked away.

Ruth chuckled at Naomi's joke about herself and turned to Lydia.

"So, you were married to Mahlon?" Lydia began the conversation.

"I was," Ruth nodded. "We had a good marriage, though it was far too short. Have you married?" Ruth asked hoping to get away from the subject of Mahlon. She had shed enough tears for a lifetime, and did not care to talk of her former husband at the moment.

"I have not, though I will be wed soon enough. Samuel has asked for my hand, and he and Father have come to an agreement. We will be wed this summer."

"That is wonderful!" Ruth exclaimed and she was sincere in her congratulations.

"Ruth, I do not mean to pry, and I mean no disrespect, so please forgive me if I am being too personal," Ruth nodded her head with a silent prayer this would not lead back to her time in marriage.

"I do not know what provisions you and Naomi have, but soon the barley fields will be ready to harvest. In our land, those of us who are not wealthy may glean from the fields after the reapers. I will not have to glean this year due to my upcoming marriage; Samuel is helping to provide for me, but I have had to for many years in times past. It is hot work, and it is tiring work, but it is profitable in that you will be able to put food on the table for yourself and for Naomi."

Ruth took in all that Lydia was explaining to her about the gleaning process and was appreciative of the wealth of information she shared. Their visit lasted for close to an hour before Lydia took her leave with a promise to return soon for another visit. Ruth continued to sit in the meadow and think for a while after Lydia departed.

She remembered the numerous fields they passed on their way to the city, and she remembered those fields being full of produce. She also remembered the reaction of the townspeople when they realized a Moabite woman would be living amongst them. How would they feel were she to show up in one of their fields and attempt to glean? Even if it was the law and permissible, she was sure to be shunned and possibly even driven away.

The kind eyes of the owner of the field outside of town flitted through her mind. Perhaps he would allow her to glean in his field? He had looked kind enough. Ruth rolled her eyes at her ownself. He probably would not even remember the simple exchange. Yet, he was the first, and besides Jedidiah's family, the only "kind eyes" she had yet to observe in Bethlehem. *Everything happens for a reason*, she remembered. Waving the thought away, Ruth decided her exhaustion was causing her to think illogically. Surely there was something she could do, somewhere she would be allowed to glean. Yet another reason to petition Jehovah, she thought.

"Dear Lord," she prayed aloud as she knelt in the meadow between the barns. "Your goodness has been overwhelming. You granted us safe passage from Moab to Bethlehem. You granted us aid when we needed it to cross the Jordan River and to complete our journey. You sent friends of Naomi's with provisions once we arrived, and the structure was all but ready when we made it here. I come to You now with gratitude and in sincere thankfulness for all You have already done, dear Jehovah. But I also come asking for your help once again. Show me what to do. Show me where to go to glean. Tell me when it is time for me to do so. Help me to be all for Naomi that she needs me to be—daughter-in-law, friend, and provider. Please do not let the fact that I am a Moabite hinder Naomi in her quest back to You. Do not let me hinder the relationships she needs to complete that journey. Whatever You ask of me, Lord, help me to complete it to the best of my abilities."

Once her prayer was done, Ruth made her way inside where Naomi was busy setting out food for their meal. Darkness had descended upon them now, but Naomi had been busy in her short time inside. She had found an old cloth and cleaned the table and two of the chairs for them to sit and partake of their meal. Two cots had been prepared for them to sleep on through the night, and two of the lamps were brightly burning thanks to the oil provided by Jedidiah's family.

The women sat and enjoyed nice helpings of dried meat that had been warmed, fresh bread and vegetables. After their fares of late, they felt as if the meal was fit for royalty. Ruth did not mention gleaning this night. Instead, she decided to wait for instruction from Jehovah. He would let her know when the time was right.

Their banter was light as they ate, each focusing on prioritizing the tasks that needed to be done in the home they now shared. They made a plan for the following day, cleared the table, prayed together thanking God for His provisions and His promises thus far, prayed for direction regarding their future here, and also prayed for acceptance of Ruth by the townspeople.

As they settled onto their individual cots for the night, both ladies noticed their hearts and their burdens seemed lighter, despite still being shrouded by questions of the unknown. God seemed closer to them here, and whether it was due to physical location or spiritual application, Naomi knew she had found a sense of peace at His feet.

Chapter Eleven

True to his word, Jedidiah and his family arrived bright and early the next morning. His wagon was loaded with boards, nails and other tools that most likely would be needed for repairs. Abigail and Lydia had been busy the night before baking loaves of bread and preparing vegetables they could eat throughout the day as they all worked together to get Naomi's house back in top shape.

"How in the Heaven's did you obtain all of these supplies?" Naomi questioned seeing the wagon heavy with any and everything they could possibly need.

"The townspeople, Naomi," he answered honestly. "None have forgotten the wisdom and instruction Elimelech was so willing to share with any and all before your journey, much less the many times he gave of your own supplies to help those who were in need," he stated as he began unloading the wagon. "We may not have been the friend to him, or to one another, that we

111

should have been during the famine, but none have forgotten the friend that he was to us." He moved closer to Naomi and lowered his voice. "I will not pretend everyone is in acceptance of Ruth "the Moabitess" being brought into our village," he spoke in quiet honesty to his dear friend, "but there is not one in the entire town who is not thrilled about you returning home," he finished.

"To accept my return," she answered plainly, "they must accept Ruth as well. I cannot thank your family enough, Jedidiah for the assistance and welcome we have received, but I will not tolerate any ill feelings toward Ruth from anyone in this village, regardless of their stature or their assistance toward me."

Jedidiah propped on a board he had just unloaded. "You have no worries about our family, Naomi, you know that. And as far as I am concerned, Moabite or not, Ruth is as much as a part of you now as Elimelech and your boys were. I will speak in defense of her to anyone who questions me. You have my word."

"Thank you, Jed," Naomi smiled taking a basket of nails and small tools from the wagon. "Now, I guess I need to be learning how to use some of these things," she spoke with uncertainty as she glared at the items packed neatly inside the basket she held.

"Nonsense," he grinned taking the basket from her. "Samuel will be here soon to assist me with repairs to the structures. Abigail and Lydia will assist you and Ruth on the inside. I know there is much work to be done in there as well."

"Thank you again, Jedidiah," Naomi smiled again as she walked away, "we will repay you."

"Having you back is repayment enough," he called back to her as she moved toward the house. "Abigail is absolutely beside herself with excitement and relief at your return. Her smile has been brighter in the past two days than it has been in years," he laughed.

Naomi made her way inside where Ruth, Abigail and Lydia were already hard at work. Abigail was busy cleaning cupboards, Ruth was tackling cobwebs, and Lydia was focusing on the floors. Naomi began to busy herself with the cooking area. She remembered when Elimelech had put this area in their home. He was so proud that he had been able to do so. Many people had to go outdoors to build fires to prepare their meals, but Naomi could do so comfortably inside their home, out of the elements. He had always been so attentive to her well-being, always attending to her comfort before his own. Tears stung her eyes at the thought of him, and she blinked them away quickly as she heard someone approaching.

"This is a fine area," Ruth commented as she knelt beside her mother-in-law, her own cloth and bucket of water in hand. "I can only imagine how many people you have fed from this cooking place," she finished, trying to engage Naomi in conversation. The older woman looked to her and smiled, forcing herself to swallow back the sob lodged in her throat.

"I can remember the meals," Abigail began pausing in her work. "Elimelech was so generous when it came to the people of our village. Naomi would often prepare his kills and a feast would be laid out for any and for all that would come. Everyone would fill their stomachs and the conversations that would ensue; honestly, he was the wisest man in our village."

Naomi was lost in thought thinking of some of those past conversations. "Naomi," Ruth spoke quietly interrupting her thoughts, "are you well?"

"Yes, dear," she nodded patting Ruth's hand. "It is still just so hard to believe how much we had here before, compared to the nothing we have now."

"It will be alright," Ruth reminded her, "Jehovah already has a plan. We just have to wait for Him to reveal it." Naomi smiled to her and shook her head to clear her mind.

"Ruth," she spoke clearing her throat and regaining her composure, "take what money we have and go into town. We shall have lentils and figs for our meal this night, and I am going to prepare them, here, in our home." She paused as she began to turn back to her task of cleaning the cooking area, seeing Abigail also halt in her task. "Lydia," Naomi continued sensing her friend's discomfort, "will you be so kind as to accompany her?" she asked.

"Certainly," Lydia agreed. "I will be happy to."

"Naomi, are you sure?" Abigail finally asked quietly, looking first to Naomi and then to Ruth.

"If Ruth can manage getting herself and an old woman across a desert, she can manage the village." Naomi spoke with a surety that surprised even herself.

"We will be fine, mother," Lydia assured her brushing dust from her apron. Abigail nodded her consent with a single nod and moved back to the task at hand.

Ruth decided to take only half of the money they had earned. She knew the generosity of Jedidiah's family could not last indefinitely, and she wanted to have something left for the future. Tying the small satchel of coins to her belt, the ladies began the walk into town. The day was pleasant, and Ruth took in the landscape around her, so different from the landscape in Moab. Here, their home rested at the top of a small knoll and from this viewpoint she could take in the fields of barley and grain in the distance below them. The blue sky above and the fields dancing in the gentle breeze below painted a picturesque scene as they walked.

Ruth sincerely enjoyed Lydia's company. So unlike Orpah, her bubbly personality and positive outlook on life gave Ruth much needed companionship. They talked of life in Bethlehem compared to life in Moab and of Lydia's upcoming wedding to Samuel, whom Ruth had met and found pleasant as well. With the lively conversation, it did not take long for the ladies to reach the town.

The city streets were crowded with people buying and selling their wares. Tents lined the alleyways with everything from household goods to handmade jewelry, from fresh vegetables to livestock and fish. Children ran through the streets enjoying their time outdoors while their mothers shopped or drew water from the well in the center of it all. Ruth noticed a shepherd herding a small flock of sheep down one alleyway, while two men bartered loudly over the "outrageous" price of a cow.

"Does this remind you of Moab?" Lydia laughed noticing how intently Ruth took everything in.

"Partially," Ruth answered though not expanding on what did and what did not remind her of her former home.

"The city is unusually crowded today," Lydia admitted. "No doubt people are gathering supplies in anticipation of the barley harvest. Let us make our purchases and be on our way."

Lydia began to navigate through the crowd, Ruth right behind her. No doubt Lydia had a certain vendor in mind, and Ruth was obliged to allow her to take the lead. They weaved calmly through person after person, navigating their way through the crowd, until a rather large man stepped in between them stopping Ruth in her tracks.

"Your money is no good here, Moabitess," he spat.

"Pardon me, sir," Ruth spoke ignoring his comment and attempting to make her way around him.

"Did you not hear me?" he spoke again, more forceful this time. "I said we do not sell to Moabites in this village. You are not welcome here!" he insisted grabbing her arm. The move surprised Ruth, and she gasped as his fingers tightened around her arm, at the same time noticing his other hand slowly going toward the sack of coins at her waist.

"If my money is no good here there is no reason for you to steal it," she spat back, her tone equally as forceful. "Release me."

Her tone and accusation surprised him, but he did not release his grip on her arm.

"Let her go, Nabal!" Lydia yelled gaining the attention of passersby.

"I will not!" he answered firmly. "We do not cater to Moabites in this town, regardless of how they weasel their way in."

"Is there a problem here?" a strong voice spoke calmly from behind him.

"Nabal is simply living up to his name," Lydia answered. Ruth could not see the man who was speaking due to the large ogre blocking her view. At the sound of the strangers' voice, the man lessened his grip and Ruth pulled free.

"Move along, Nabal," the stranger continued, "money is money regardless of who holds it," he finished.

The man called Nabal scoffed at Ruth but slowly moved around her. She did not miss the blasphemies he uttered under his breath as he passed by her. Ruth watched as others, women mostly, stared at her as they continued to brush past. None of them bothered to ask of her well-being, attempt to console her, or even to cast a sorrowful eye in her direction. No one could care less; besides Lydia.

"Are you alright? How about your arm?" she asked sincerely rushing to her friends' side, examining her arm for bruises.

"My arm is fine," Ruth answered honestly.

"Lydia, I do not mean to sound unkind, but I suggest you take your new friend, collect whatever it is you came to town for, and get yourselves out of the village. People are not used to a Moabite being among them, and the streets are full of opinions today," the stranger advised meeting the eyes of the glaring passersby.

Ruth noticed him for the first time.

"Thank you for your assistance, Ezra," Lydia spoke kindly from Ruth's side. "We shall hurry."

Ruth muttered a thank you as well, and though she appreciated the kindness of his gesture in freeing her from the man called Nabal, she was not sure he comfortably accepted her presence among them either. Just because he would not tolerate a man being unkind to a woman did not mean that he welcomed her, a Moabitess, into his town. He simply bowed his head in her direction as she passed and moved on his way.

Though there were no more physical encounters or outright rude comments as they passed, Ruth still noticed how uncomfortable she made everyone feel by being in their town. Lydia kept hold of her arm for the rest of their time there, and moved quickly to the tents where she knew there would be no trouble.

With the money they had brought and with a small contribution from Lydia, Ruth was able to purchase lentils and figs as Naomi had requested, as well as a few fish from one of the local fishermen. The vendors seemed to have no trouble accepting her money, though each of them asked for proof that she could pay before they would hand over the food she requested.

The women could not escape the town fast enough, and Ruth could almost feel the tension easing with each step she took away from the villagers.

"Ruth, I am so sorry for the treatment you endured today, but I must say I am not surprised," Lydia said breaking the silence. "Our people do not accept outsiders well at any rate, but Moab is not a place known for honesty and integrity. They just assume you possess the same nature. They will see, as time goes on, that you are not like most of the Moabites we have encountered."

"And how many Moabites have you encountered?" Ruth surprised her by asking. Lydia stopped in her tracks considering the question. Ruth continued. "I do not try to defend

119

the ways and the practices of Moab. And I do not pretend that the people there are not calloused and hard, and some of them are, yes, full of evil, as no doubt so are some people here. But cultural differences should not determine the character of a person. A person cannot help where they are born or where they come from, but they can change the way they are and in what direction they are going." Ruth was not angry in the words she said, nor were they directed specifically at Lydia, but she made her point plainly and politely.

"You are right, Ruth, and I apologize for the actions of my people," she began. "However, I can truthfully say that I do not care where you came from; I only care for the person who stands before me now." The ladies hugged, broke their embrace, and continued on their way.

"Do you think I will be permitted to glean in the fields around Bethlehem as you told me about?" Ruth asked honestly as they continued on their way. "Do not get me wrong, I am not fearful, but I also do not wish to be thrown from a field. I will do what I have to, but I would rather avoid embarrassment, if possible," she chuckled.

"It is a law that you be allowed to glean, but I will not pretend you may not face some contention. Just trust in Jehovah to lead you where you need to go."

The ladies agreed not to share the encounter with Nabal with their families. There was no use in causing more worry among them. The meal that night was delightful. Naomi cooked the fish and lentils to perfection and the small assembly had their fill. Stories were shared of the journey to and from Moab, and Ruth learned of life in Bethlehem before Elimelech took his family away.

When Jedidiah and his family left that evening, the home had taken on a whole new atmosphere. No more boards were hanging askew outside from wind and neglect, and no more cobwebs hung from the inside corners. A warm fire danced in the cooking area, filling the room with a comfortable glow. Two of the rooms beyond the main area had been cleaned and made ready for sleeping. Ruth would take the room which had once been Mahlon's, and Naomi had decided, after much thought, that she would resume her former room, the room she had shared with Elimelech.

"It was a good day," Ruth spoke breaking the silence, when it was only the two of them in the house once again.

"Yes, it was," Naomi agreed. "We could not have done it without the assistance of Jed and his precious family," she continued. "I do not know what we would have done without them."

"Just more proof of what you have taught me," Ruth reminded her, "that Jehovah will provide for every need."

Naomi smiled and looked to her daughter-in-law. "You are right," she agreed. "Still, sometimes His divine intervention even surprises me," she admitted.

Ruth crossed to where her mother-in-law sat and knelt at her feet. "We cannot continue to expect, nor accept, such charity from Jedidiah's family. They have little themselves as you have told me. We must make our own way, and we need to do so sooner rather than later."

"What do you propose," Naomi asked looking skeptical though intrigued. She knew Ruth was getting around to something, she just was not sure what.

"Lydia has told me of the laws of your people that the poor, *and foreigners* she stressed, be allowed to glean in the fields. The barley harvest has begun. Let me now go to the field, and glean ears of corn after him in whose sight I might find grace."

Naomi looked at the young woman at her feet. She could barely process such an innocent and humble soul. This woman, Moabite or not, had lost everything when she lost her husband, had given up any rights she still may have had as a widow in Moab and any hope of a future she could have possibly obtained there, and thrown all of that aside to care for an old woman. An old woman who had once had more than she could ever dream of having, yet had foolishly allowed her husband to take her to a far country, and lost everything while they were there.

She laid her withered hand on Ruth's beautiful face. Ruth was right. She was wise beyond her years, and she spoke with wisdom and a humility Naomi only wished she, herself could possess.

"Go my daughter," she agreed. "May Jehovah lead and guide you," she finished. Ruth laid her head on Naomi's knees.

"We are going to be fine, I promise," she spoke without raising her head. "I will ready myself in the morning and seek the field where Jehovah will lead me," she promised.

Naomi bent and kissed the top of her head. Ruth raised herself and moved to the room where she would take her rest. She leaned against the wall and took a deep breath to steady her nerves. Tomorrow she would wander out alone and seek a field in which to reap. "Jehovah, please be my guide," she whispered. The she lowered herself to her cot and slept peacefully for the first night in years.

Chapter Twelve

Ruth was up before the sun the next morning, and was surprised that Naomi was already hard at work with a steaming pot of porridge simmering in the cooking area. Ruth greeted the older woman with a smile as she took her place at the table in the center of the room.

"You are awake early this morning," she stated as Naomi sat a steaming bowl in front of her. "This smells wonderful," she spoke truthfully taking in the aroma of the food before her.

"You will need strength for the day, Ruth," Naomi spoke with surety as she laid a cake of bread in the center of the table. "The work will be hard, and the day will be long. Do not be discouraged if you are not met with kind words and welcoming arms," Naomi spoke honestly. "The law is clear that the poor and foreigners be allowed to glean, but that does not mean that all the citizens of our land are in favor of it," she spoke truthfully. Ruth took in all that

Naomi was saying to her. Naomi paused long enough for them to give thanks for the food and then began again.

"I am not sure of the laws of gleaning in Moab, but I want to make sure you understand the requirements and the laws here in Bethlehem." Ruth listened intently. "The barley stalks will be cut off and all the ears of grain will be picked from them. The produce will then be piled into stacks called sheaves. Workers will eventually thresh those sheaves to get the grain out of the plants. You are not allowed to walk among the piles of these sheaves that have been pulled or to collect anything there on the ground. What you will be allowed to pull from are the standing stalks which remain in the corners of the field and of any that the reapers miss along their way. Many will be in Bethlehem today as well, gleaning after the reapers. Our crops are full this year and people will come from neighboring villages and cities to take advantage of that. If the first field you come to looks to be filled with gleaners, go a bit further. And again, do not be discouraged if you are able to obtain only a very little. God provided manna for our ancestors on a daily basis during the wanderings; if you are able to only obtain enough for one meal, that will be sufficient for the need at hand," she encouraged her.

Ruth nodded as she took another bite of bread. "I will do my very best, Naomi," she promised.

"I know you will, daughter, and even if you come back empty handed, God will provide enough to sustain our needs this night," Naomi acknowledged. "Use this to gather what you can," Naomi continued, handing Ruth a small basket.

Ruth laughed at the size. "This should be easy to fill," she laughed as she put her arm through the handle.

"I do not want you to be disappointed," Naomi grinned. "Fill this basket, and it will be more than plenty," she chuckled. "But care for it," she continued. "This basket was woven by my grandmother. I have cherished it for years," she admitted. She handed Ruth the beautiful basket carefully woven so many years ago. The craftsmanship was beautiful. Ruth was amazed that Naomi would trust her with it.

"I promise to protect it with my life," Ruth assured her dramatically as she exited the door. "I shall return soon!" she yelled over her shoulder.

"God be with you, daughter," Naomi called back to her from her place at the door.

Ruth looked back as she continued on her way and could still see Naomi watching her leave until she crossed over the knoll and their home was out of sight. From her vantage point above them, she could see fields full of reapers and gleaners. She thought she had gotten an early start, but clearly, the crowds had descended upon Bethlehem early. With another prayer for guidance, she continued on her way.

It did not take long before she approached the first field. She slowed in her steps but did not move beyond the stalks just yet. Voices drifted to her ears, and she slowed to listen when she heard her name spoken.

"Ruth, her name is Ruth," the unknown speaker continued. It was a female voice. "I am not sure how she convinced Mahlon to marry her, but apparently, he did. Of course, who else would he have married in Moab but a Moabitess. It is not as if the land was filled with fine Israeli women."

"But look what happened!" another voice cut in. "All of the men lost their lives, and now Naomi has lost everything, returned home poor and destitute, and has brought her, a Moabite, into our village!"

"I do not know what she was thinking of by bringing her back with her to Bethlehem, but *Ruth*" the first voice emphasized, "will never be accepted here."

Ruth stopped but stayed hidden from view. "I do not know," another female voice chimed in, "that seems a bit harsh, there has to be something decent to her. I mean, she left everything to get Naomi back here safely."

"Would you not do anything you could to escape Moab?" the first voice questioned.

"Well, I would not have been there to begin with," the once defending voice retaliated. The three females laughed together, and Ruth continued moving forward. This was surely not a field she felt led to glean in.

She continued on her way until she came to the field that she remembered so vividly from the day they arrived in Bethlehem. The field of "the owner with kind eyes," she smiled to herself remembering the odd exchange.

This one, she almost heard, feeling a nudge from within. Though she knew that the law required the Jewish people to allow the poor and foreigners to glean in their fields, she felt kindness was always the best approach. She entered the stalks and looked around until she saw a man who seemed to be overseeing the reapers. He stood tall and proud with a watchful eye as he took in all that was going on around him.

His back was to Ruth as she approached, and though she noticed a few of the reapers pause in their task as she passed, none of them gave any more than a glance in her direction before going back to their work. At least no one was gossiping aloud about her that she could hear.

"Excuse me, sir," she began as she drew nearer to the man. She continued to speak as he turned to face her. "I pray you, let me glean and gather after the reapers among the sheaves," she asked as humbly as she knew how. Her surprise came when the man turned to face her.

"Ruth," he began matter-of-factly, "the Moabitess damsel who returned with Naomi, I believe?" he questioned.

"Yes, kind sir, it is I," she acknowledged, unable to believe it was Ezra who was standing before her. "I want to thank you again for your assistance in the marketplace," she continued.

Ezra smiled a genuine smile, easing her fears of being completely rejected. "You may glean," he continued motioning for her to begin in the far corner of the field. Ruth could feel the tension leaving her shoulders.

The reapers here were very efficient, but plenty was left for the gleaners. Those in positions, much like herself, were working feverishly, and though Ruth could hear some friendly talk and even light banter here and there, everyone in this field seemed so content with their positions that they cared not that a foreigner was among them.

"Welcome, to Bethlehem," one young lady spoke to her as she worked. "I am Mary," she continued smiling in Ruth's direction. She did not pause in her work but continued in close proximity to Ruth. This woman was most certainly an employed reaper, and Ruth was surprised she was being spoken to by one of the hired hands. She accepted the kind gesture and returned the salutation.

"Hello, Mary," Ruth returned. "I am Ruth. It is a pleasure to meet you," she smiled as she too continued her work.

"Ezra was surprised at your asking permission to glean," Mary went on. "Most just arrive in the field and begin taking what the law allows, never thinking to seek approval," she stated.

"I was aware that the law permitted foreigners and the poor to glean, but I felt it would be more polite to ask the owner's permission first," Ruth admitted. "I do not wish to take advantage of the laws or of the owner," she spoke truthfully.

"Oh, Ezra is not the owner," Mary clarified. "He is, in fact, the overseer of this field, but he is not the owner. Boaz is the owner." Ruth paused, her hand over an ear of corn in mid-air. Mary recognized her discomfort and continued quickly. "No, it is alright," she continued. "Ezra is exactly who you should have spoken to. Boaz trusts him fully and is completely confident in his decisions. You did exactly as you should have," she assured her, "and more than was expected," she finished.

Ruth thought back suddenly to the day they arrived in Bethlehem and had passed this field. She had remembered then seeing two men talking. She had assumed then that the owner was praising the overseer, which would make perfect sense that Ezra was the one receiving the praise. Ruth shook her head at her forgetfulness but continued with her task. Ezra had given her permission, and Mary seemed to think that was sufficient.

The morning was hot, but Ruth continued in the job while talking and laughing throughout the day with her new friend, Mary. The sun was high in the sky when a bell was rung signifying it was break time for the reapers. Ruth was surprised when the gleaners also paused their work.

"Come," Mary encouraged her. "Rest your back and have some water," she instructed. Ruth was reluctant, curious as to how others would view her taking a place among them, but moved in the direction Mary led her when she saw all the other gleaners were doing the same. Buckets of water and crackers, along with dried pieces of meat and cheese, were spread across large blankets under huge tents that had been placed beneath trees which bowed almost to the ground, kindly lending shade from their branches. A welcome reprieve to any and all who were willing to rest beneath them.

Ruth was surprised the gleaners were treated as kindly as the reapers and were encouraged to partake in, not only the shade, but the provisions as well. She moved reluctantly inside the tent and was equally surprised at the smiles and salutations that were directed her way. A few were only following suit of their peers, that was obvious, but most of the people here were being genuinely kind to her.

Ezra made his way among them and spoke to them all as a group. "You have done well this morning," he announced. "Jehovah has provided a bountiful crop this year, and thanks to each of you, if the weather holds, this field will be cleared in record time. Take your rest, then keep up the good work," he commended them with a smile and a nod. Ruth noticed the silent exchange that took place between Ezra and Mary as he passed.

"Is there something you should tell me?" she chided her friend. Mary handed her a cracker with a small piece of dried meat and cheese. She smiled and her face flushed.

"Perhaps," she admitted with a sheepish grin. "We shall see when Ezra speaks to my father after the harvest is complete."

Ruth's eyebrows met her hairline, and her smile lit her face. "Mary that is wonderful!" she exclaimed, truly happy for her new friend.

"It is surprising," Mary continued, "that Ezra would notice me. I began as a gleaner like yourself, a few years back, but this year I was hired on as a reaper. You will not find kindness in other fields as you will find in the ones owned by Boaz. I just happened to find the right field, with the right man!" she finished, looking to Ezra. He met her eyes and returned the smile.

Ruth adored the simple exchange. "There is no such thing as happenstance," she laughed. "Jehovah led you to this field as He did me. I passed others, but none felt right until I came to this one. I have been treated with such kindness here, and I cannot thank you enough," she concluded.

"I am thankful that you feel that way," Mary continued. "I can tell that Ezra is impressed with your work. The barley harvest will continue for about two months, and then the wheat will be ready. It is hard work, but your family will reap the benefits. We appreciate good gleaners, they make our job easier," she admitted.

Ruth cast her eyes at the ground where she sat. *Her family.* The word resonated in her ears. Just a little while ago there were five in her family. Now there was only two. How empty she felt sometimes. Mary noticed the change in her disposition.

"Ruth, are you well? Did I say something wrong?" her friend asked.

"No, not at all," Ruth quickly reassured her. She shook her head, removing the discouraging thoughts from her mind, and smiled a genuine smile. "Jehovah just continues to be so good to me," she spoke truthfully, though she was saying so to remind herself as much as she was for the benefit of Mary.

"He has to us all," Mary agreed passing the pitcher of water to Ruth, who drank appreciatively. The two ladies continued in easy conversation, and others joined in. It was such a welcome change from the reception Ruth had expected. Their conversation was so pleasant, Ruth did not notice when another approached the field until his voice cut through the air.

"The Lord be with you," his deep voice exclaimed as he approached.

"The Lord bless thee," all of the reapers repeated together, extending greetings in his direction. Saluting them all, he moved to Ezra where the men began exchanging, what appeared to be, pleasant conversation.

Ruth recognized him as the man she had seen the day they came to Bethlehem. *This must be Boaz,* she thought to herself.

As if reading her mind, Mary echoed her thoughts. "That is Boaz," she affirmed, "the owner of this and many other fields in Bethlehem. And he is one of the kindest owners you will ever meet," she spoke with surety. "Many women have attempted to catch his eye, but none have succeeded. He would be quite the catch," Mary admitted teasingly.

Ruth looked away from him just before he caught sight of her and looked back to her friend. "I cannot imagine ever loving another as I loved Mahlon," Ruth spoke with sincerity "and you are forgetting that Boaz is a very wealthy Israelite man, and I am nothing but a poor, Moabite widow with no hope of a kinsman redeemer," she spoke honestly. "Nevertheless, Jehovah will care for me as He has been doing."

Mary smiled to her friend, sorry that she had teased her and glad that she had not been overly rebuked for it.

Boaz, meanwhile, unknowing to the two women who had captured his attention, was captivated. *Who is that woman sitting among my reapers. There's something familiar about her. Have I seen this woman before*, he thought to himself. Never in all his years had he seen such a beautiful woman, and finally, he could keep his questions to himself no longer.

"Whose damsel is this?" he questioned Ezra quietly as they continued their conversation out of earshot of the others.

Ezra smiled at Boaz's reaction to her. She was a beautiful girl, but Ezra had also observed that there was much more to Ruth than physical beauty, an observation he was more than happy to share with his employer, who also happened to be one of his dearest friends.

"It is the Moabitess damsel that came back with Naomi out of the country of Moab. She came to me this morning and said, 'I pray you, let me glean and gather after the reapers among the sheaves.' So she came, and hath continued even from the morning until now, that she tarried a little in the house."

"And her name?" Boaz inquired.

"Her name is Ruth," Ezra answered working to keep the smile from his face. He had seen many maidens cross the fields of his employer. Many of those maidens had attempted to gain the attention of Boaz, and though he had witnessed nothing but kindness from Boaz toward any of them, no woman had ever piqued his interest as this one seemed to.

"Yes, I have heard of this, Ruth," Boaz admitted, testing the name on his lips. He had heard the story of Naomi's return to Bethlehem just this morning and of the circumstances which had led to her return.

Boaz continued to stare at Ruth, and his heart literally skipped a beat when she laughed quietly at whatever Mary was sharing with her.

"Has she been treated unkindly here?" he continued to question Ezra, still staring at this woman who had so captivated him. He knew how some felt about a Moabitess being in their village, he had heard that talk in town as well, but he would tolerate nothing but kindness to anyone in any of his fields.

"Not here in your field, no," he began, "though I did stop an altercation in the market yesterday."

"An altercation?" Boaz broke his trance and looked sharply at his friend, his look demanding an explanation.

"Nabal," Ezra stated, and though no more needed to be said, he continued. "Ruth, along with Jedidiah's daughter, Lydia, were there, I assume to gather supplies. Nabal had taken Ruth by the arm and was demanding her to leave. He said Moabites were not welcome in Bethlehem and that her money was no good here. However, she was holding her own," he continued quickly, amused just thinking about how sweet, little Ruth was standing up to the rude man twice her size. "She called him out for attempting to steal her money pouch and demanded that he release her."

"Did he harm her?" Boaz asked through clenched teeth.

Ezra had clearly been amused, but now that he saw how serious his employer had become, he quickly answered solemnly in all seriousness and truth.

"He did not harm her. He did not release her until I demanded it, but then he went about his way. I instructed Lydia to get what they needed quickly and then return to Naomi's home."

"Of course, she would be in danger in town," Boaz chewed on the corner of his mustache, something he typically only did when he was in deep consideration over something personal. After only a moment's thought he voiced clear instructions to his overseer.

"No one is to touch her here," he instructed looking to Ezra.

Ezra nodded his understanding and watched as Boaz looked once again to Ruth who was now standing and about to go back into the field. Boaz quickly made his way to where she and Mary stood, and Mary paused seeing him approaching behind Ruth. Ruth felt a presence behind her, and noticing Mary's awkward gaze, looked over her shoulder as she turned slowly to stare up into the face of the handsome man who owned the field where she had found herself just this morning.

For a moment, Ruth feared the worst. She feared that all the kindness Mary had professed this man possessed did not extend to Moabite women. She knew she was about to be thrown from the field and told never to return. All of her hard work this morning had been in vain and all of the hope she had allowed to creep into her heart was about to be crushed, until he spoke.

His eyes were kind, and his face was soft as he began to speak to her. "Hearest thou not, my daughter? Go not to glean in another field, neither go from hence, but abide here fast by my maidens: Let thine eyes be on the field that they do reap, and go thou after them: have I not charged the young men that they shall not touch thee? and when thou art athirst, go unto the vessels and drink of that which the young men have drawn."

Ruth stared into his eyes. She felt as if he were looking into the depths of her very soul. Mary did not speak but simply laid her hand on Ruth's arm bringing her back to reality. At her touch, Ruth fell to her knees, bowing before him.

"Why have I found grace in thine eyes, that thou shouldest take knowledge of me, seeing I am a stranger?" she cried unable to hold back her emotions. She wet his feet with her tears. This man whom she had just imagined throwing her from his property was expanding goodness and kindness on her in more ways than she thought possible. Boaz did not allow her to stay at his feet. He bent down touching both her shoulders to gain her attention, then reached for her hands. A wave went through his body as she carefully placed her hands in his. Assisting her to stand, he spoke even more gentle than before, but with no less feeling or emotion.

"It hath fully been shewed me, all that thou hast done unto thy mother-in-law since the death of thine husband: and how thou hast left thy father and thy mother, and the land of thy nativity, and art come unto a people which thou knewest not heretofore. The LORD recompense thy work, and a full reward be given thee of the

LORD God of Israel, under whose wings thou art come to trust."

Ruth stood before him, a single tear escaping again down her cheek. She realized then that he still held her hands gently in his own. Pulling away she wiped the tears from her face with her head covering. She realized instantly that they were quite the spectacle as every reaper, gleaner, and foreman in their presence stared at the scene they were causing. Ruth gathered herself before she spoke again, but her words continued to hold every ounce of humility and gratitude that she could convey.

"Let me find favour in thy sight, my lord; for thou hast comforted me, and for that thou hast spoken friendly unto thine handmaid, though I be not like unto one of thine handmaidens," she bowed her head again in appreciation for his kindness and turned to go back into the field. She stopped when she heard him speak her name.

"Ruth," she turned again to face him, "At mealtime come thou hither, and eat of the bread, and dip thy morsel in the vinegar."

She acknowledged his request with a simple bow of her head.

"I shall, my lord," she promised. As she approached the field once again, Mary beside her though not yet speaking a word of all that had transpired, Ruth looked back over her shoulder to see Boaz continuing to watch her. She smiled a small smile, then picked up her basket, almost filled, and continued the task she had come to do.

Boaz turned back to Ezra as a huge smile spread across his face. Ezra stared at the man in front of him, shocked at all that had just transpired. Ruth was extremely kind, yes. She was a beautiful damsel and a hard worker, yes. She would be an asset to employ as a reaper, yes. But Boaz was utterly smitten with this Moabite widow. Ezra was more than fine with that, but what about the others in their village. When they found out Boaz had forbidden anyone to touch her, when word got out that he had invited her to dine with them, if others saw him look at Ruth the way Ezra had seen him look at her, would those realizations be bad for business? She was a Moabitess after all.

Ezra knew better than to question this man he so respected, but when Boaz spoke again, Ezra thought he had clearly taken leave of his senses. Boaz turned to the men remaining in his presence and spoke in a firm voice loud enough for each of them to hear and to clearly understand.

"Let her glean even among the sheaves, and reproach her not; And let fall also some handfuls of purpose for her, and leave them, that she may glean them, and rebuke her not."

Boaz laughed aloud at the faces he saw before him. Clearly, he had stunned them into silence.

"No," he continued, "to answer the questions playing in your minds, I have not lost my senses," he assured them. "This damsel, Ruth, has gone through much and has nothing, yet the tender care and love she has and continues to bestow upon her mother-in-law, Naomi is unheard of. This woman has lost her husband, she has left her father and mother and the land she called home to bring Naomi back to us, and she, most importantly, has turned from the pagan gods of Moab to our God, the one true God, Jehovah. That will not go unrewarded. I will be back at mealtime, and until then, heed all I have said," he finished as he turned to go.

The men watched him leave and then looked to Ezra. The tune Boaz whistled as he walked rang in their ears. Ezra scratched his head and then turned to look at the men who looked to him for direction.

"You heard the boss," he stated empathically. "Get back to work."

Chapter Thirteen

As instructed, the reapers and gleaners went quickly back to work. Ruth was not surprised at the stares she received after the events that had taken place. Though things had happened so quickly it all seemed rather surreal to her. She saw Ezra talking with Mary, and witnessed Mary's smile as she approached her once again.

"What?" Ruth asked innocently still not completely clear of all that had happened.

"Come with me," Mary instructed. Ruth followed her from her place near the corner of the field in amongst the piles of sheaves that had been so strategically placed along the outskirts of the field. Ruth watched as the men picked up the heavy bundles, and repeatedly dropped handfuls of the grains on the ground.

"What is all this?" she questioned Mary who continued to smile at her with her arms folded tightly across her chest.

"A poor, Moabite widow you may be," she repeated Ruth's own words to her, "but one which has captured the attention of the most eligible bachelor in all the village," she smiled. Ruth continued to look at her in confusion. "Boaz has instructed that you are to glean among the sheaves we have gathered," Mary clarified. "And he has instructed that handfuls of grain be 'dropped' for your benefit," she finished.

Ruth stared at the scene before and was quite certain she would be banned from all society after this. She laughed to herself at the goodness of God. Forgetting her earlier comment to Mary regarding happenstance, she could not help but wonder, how in the world, out of all of the fields in Bethlehem, did she happen to land in the field of a man like Boaz?

"Come on," Mary continued laughing at Ruth's overwhelmed state, I shall help you gather the spoils and show you how to thresh the barley so that you can carry more with you," she encouraged her. "We have more baskets you may take home as well."

"But I cannot accept more generosity from you, Mary. I do not wish to cause trouble among you and the other reapers," Ruth continued.

"You have nothing to worry about," Mary promised her. "Ezra will take care of me. Jehovah, and Boaz, have chosen this day to take care of you. Do not rob Boaz of this blessing," she instructed. "You have made quite the impression on him. We must hurry, the evening meal will be served soon, and you promised him you would be there."

The ladies began threshing and filling basket after basket with grain. There was so much that Ruth wondered if she would be able to carry it all home. The sun had moved across the sky when the reapers began to end their day and the gleaners began to go their separate ways, taking their earnings with them.

Mary and Ruth joined the other reapers under a large tent where they each took a seat around a large table. The aroma of fresh baked bread filled the area and Ruth's stomach rumbled at the scent. Bowls of vinegar and olive oil were placed strategically across the tables so that each and every one could enjoy them and have their fill. Boaz made sure Ruth was able to enjoy each and every dish he had to offer. Time and again he passed her flavorful oils and vinegars, ripe olives, which were among her favorites, and a true delicacy, parched corn. Until now, Ruth had never tasted such a dish. She was careful not to take more than would be considered polite, and she savored every morsel.

The day was drawing to an end when Ruth took her leave. Mary helped her arrange the baskets across her back and arms and Boaz made sure she had plenty of time to get home before the sun would set. She thanked them all for their generosity, help, and kindness, time and again, and was only given her leave when she vowed that she would return the next day.

Despite her heavy load, her steps home were light and full of promise. Ruth sang praises to Jehovah part of the way, caring not if anyone heard her, and laughed as her load begin weighing on her for the second part of her journey. She did not feel she could get home fast enough and could not wait for Naomi to see her earnings and to tell her of the blessings the day had held. Mary had also packed an extra cake of bread, a small cruse of oil and even a small serving of the parched corn that Ruth had loved so much for Naomi. She had also included a small bag of olives for Ruth, noticing how she loved the fruits so much. Boaz, in all of his kindness, had made Ruth feel like royalty.

She began to call for Naomi as she reached the top of the knoll that she now called home.

"Naomi, come and see the blessings of Jehovah!" she shouted loud enough for the world to hear. Anyone who was in earshot would have no doubt that joy had come to Ruth this day. She only called out twice before Naomi opened the door to their dwelling. The old woman's eyes were as big as her face when she beheld Ruth coming toward her.

"Where hast thou gleaned to day? And where wroughtest thou? Blessed be he that did take knowledge of thee," Naomi spoke in awe as she met Ruth in front of the house and attempted to take some of her load.

"Naomi, wait until I tell you of the most wonderful and blessed experience I have had this day!" Ruth all but sang the words. "I met the most wonderful people, Naomi," she began. "Wait until you see what they have sent."

"I see what they have sent," she exclaimed while continuing to "un-pack" her daughter-in-law. "My dear, you are loaded with as much as a beast of burden would be expected to haul! How did you carry all of this all this way?"

"Jehovah guided my steps and gave me the strength, Naomi." The women had made their way inside the house, and Ruth had finally settled her load on the floor and on the table in the center of the room. She took a deep breath and then led Naomi to a seat at the table. "Here is your great-grandmother's basket," she smiled as she produced the basket she had so carefully protected, "and look at what is inside!" She sat out the cruz of oil, the cake of bread, and the parched corn. "It was the most wonderful day, Naomi," she began again as she unwrapped the goods. And you have never tasted anything as delicious as this," she promised excitedly as she handed her the parched corn.

Naomi took in everything that was being shown to her. She could not believe Jehovah had provided so much for them in just one day. She blessed the food Ruth had placed before her and dipped the bread into the oil. She closed her eyes as the morsel hit her tongue. It had been years since she had tasted olive oil, and Ruth was right, never had she tasted anything as delicious as the parched corn. She knew immediately that Ruth had not happened upon an everyday farmer's field. She knew that Ruth had not "happened upon" anything at all. It was Jehovah who had led her to this place, whatever field it was.

As Naomi ate, Ruth continued to chatter about everything that had taken place. She told Naomi of Ezra, which meant she had to divulge the information she had kept from her mother-in-law about the events in the marketplace the day before. She continued her story, telling her of her new friend, Mary, and her hope of a coming union with Ezra.

She then began to speak about "him." "He" who had spoken so kindly to her, insisting that she glean among the sheaves his reapers had cut. She told Naomi of the conversation they had that no man was to lay a hand on her in the fields, that she had been invited to dine with him and those he employed, and that he insisted she return to his field the next day to glean alongside his maidens. When she finished Ruth was exhausted, the excitement of the day and the tremendous amount of work she had done catching up with her.

"Ruth, Jehovah has indeed blessed us this day," Naomi laughed as she began to clear the table. Ruth jumped up to assist though every bone in her body had begun to ache. "Stop right there," Naomi insisted. "I will do the clearing; you will find your rest." Ruth smiled but did not have it in her to argue this evening. She sat back down at her place at the table, her legs and back protesting every move she made. "You have told me of everything and of everyone who was so openly kind to you this day, but you have not told me the name of the man who owned the field," Naomi spoke as she worked. "The man who was so extremely kind and seems to have taken such an interest in you," Naomi added as she carried the bowls from the table to the wash basin.

"The man's name with whom I wrought today," Ruth spoke as a yawn escaped her, "is Boaz."

Naomi stopped in her tracks, the bowl she was carrying crashing to the floor. Ruth jumped in alarm and rushed to her side.

"Naomi! What is it! Are you ok?" Ruth asked taking her arm and guiding her to the nearest chair. "Are you ill?"

Naomi's face had gone pale, and her hands shook. The old woman took a deep breath and blinked her eyes to focus on the beautiful face at her knees in front of her. Carefully she lifted her hands to frame Ruth's small face.

"Who did you say?" Naomi questioned slowly, certain that she had misunderstood.

"Boaz," Ruth stated again. "His name is Boaz."

Naomi closed her eyes. She seemed to be uttering a quick and simple prayer before she stood so quickly that Ruth almost toppled backward. She raised her hands to Jehovah as tears began to stream down her withered face. Ruth watched in awe, not sure of what was happening.

"Blessed be he of the LORD, who hath not left off his kindness to the living and to the dead," Naomi almost shouted. "Ruth, this is the most wonderful news!" she continued. "How could I have been so foolish! How have I forgotten!" she continued. Suddenly she rushed to Ruth, still kneeling on the floor. Naomi took her arms as she stood, looking into Ruth's eyes. "The man is near of kin unto us, one of our next kinsmen!" she finished excitedly.

Ruth was certain her mother-in-law's mind had taken leave of her. She stood, staring at the tear-streaked face of the woman before her, thinking on what Naomi had just announced. Apparently, her family had known the family of Boaz before they left for Moab, and apparently, they were close to the family.

Naomi realized that Ruth did not entirely understand the customs of her people. She also understood that Ruth was new to their beliefs and still had much to learn concerning the laws of Jehovah.

Ruth spoke first, breaking the awkward silence. "He said unto me also, 'Thou shalt keep fast by my young men, until they have ended all my harvest'," Ruth finished.

Naomi's mind raced. Ruth watched as the woman walked around the room, obviously deep in thought and prayer. Naomi knew she must move slowly and carefully concerning this. Jehovah was at work; the bounty Boaz had heaped upon Ruth this day was apparent in that. She must be careful not get ahead of His will and

His timing. She also understood by the recent comment Ruth had said Boaz had made, that he recognized the danger Ruth could be in after he had showered her with such a bounty. Many maidens would love to be in Ruth's place as far as Boaz was concerned and would not take kindly to have been jilted for a Moabitess. She approached Ruth again; her thoughts calm and herself collected.

"It is good, my daughter, that thou go out with his maidens, that they meet thee not in any other field," she clarified. "Follow the commands given you by Boaz. Stay close to him, to Ezra, to Mary, to those whom you know you can trust." Ruth watched her carefully wondering what exactly she was thinking. She knew her mother-in-law to be careful and wise, but she felt as if Naomi was keeping something from her. Ruth respected the older woman far too much to question her and instead simply promised that she would do so. Naomi dismissed her then, admitting that she needed time alone in prayer.

Ruth stretched across the cot in her room, knowing her day tomorrow may not be as exciting as the events of today. Her body was tired and ached, and there was still much work to be done. The grain she had brought home today would go a long way, but it would take much more to get them through the winter. Fortunately, she knew exactly where to go tomorrow to glean, and she knew what would be expected of her when she arrived there.

She could not help but wonder if Boaz would make an appearance again tomorrow. She thought of his kind eyes and the way in which he had spoken to her. He seemed to be such a generous man, and his family must have been very close to the family of Elimelech. But then again, Naomi had said he was one of their "next kinsmen" whatever that meant.

She closed her eyes, and her mind went back to his touch when he had taken her hands in his to assist her from the floor. Their hands had touched again at the table, on more than one occasion, as he passed her bowl after bowl of oils and vinegars. She could not deny the shock his touch sent through her, and that she had felt that shock all the way to her shoulders.

Suddenly her eyes popped open as Mahlon came to her mind. Was she disrespecting his memory by favoring another man in such a way? She asked Jehovah for forgiveness if she had done so. Ruth knew that to survive it would be ideal for her to marry again someday, but should that be a marriage of convenience only? Would she ever be allowed to love again?

She was being ridiculous, clearly over-exhausted. Why would things so foolish even cross her mind? Boaz was simply being kind because of his familial connection to the family of Elimelech and because of the kindness she had bestowed upon Naomi. He was a wealthy landowner who could have any maiden he desired. He would never cast his lot with a Moabite widow.

Boaz lay in his chambers thinking over the events of the day. Sleep eluded him, for every time he closed his eyes, his thoughts drifted to a raven-haired damsel with eyes which seemed to search his soul. Soul-searching, that is what he needed. He had never been so taken with a woman before. Sure, maidens had caught his eye, every year at harvest time his fields were filled with them, but never had one intrigued him as this woman had.

He replayed the day's activities again in his mind. He had been attending to business in town. He had heard the tragic events that had brought Naomi back to Bethlehem, and he had heard of the Moabite who had returned with her—one of her sons' widow. Being the man he was, Boaz's heart went out to the family, and he wondered what had become of the other son's wife, the one who remained in Moab. Nevertheless, it was Ruth who was here in Bethlehem, and it was Ruth who had captured his attention. It was Ruth who had forsaken the gods of her people for the God of Israel.

He thought of her and reminded himself that Ruth had recently lost her husband of at least ten years. That alone could not be easy, but on top of that, she was now poor, destitute, hurting and alone, yet all the while, her attitude seemed to be pleasant, polite and caring. Everything she had done and all she had left behind to care for Naomi spoke volumes of how much Ruth must have loved her husband. Would her heart ever be open to love another? And why would she choose him? He was quite a bit older than Ruth after all.

Boaz was also aware of something he was certain Ruth did not know nor did she understand. He was a kinsman of Elimelech. Boaz ran his fingers through his unruly hair, sitting up on his cot. This woman had truly and utterly captivated him. The fact that she was a Moabitess did not bother him in the least, he could care less where she was from, it was her character which identified her person. He would never pressure her into a relationship, but he would work to know her better. He would protect her while she was in his presence. He would make sure that she was content while in his fields. He would make sure Naomi was cared for in all the ways he could, and he would cherish each moment Jehovah allowed him to be in her presence. Regardless of how long that might be.

Chapter Fourteen

The days which followed were pleasant for Ruth, though extremely tiring. Each morning she would make her way to the field of Boaz, glean in the company of his hired hands, take the evening meal with him and his those he employed, and return home to Naomi with loads of goods that he had so lavishly bestowed upon them. For the most part, Ruth was only met with pleasant conversation by those working alongside her in the field. However, there were a few maidens who cast leery eyes and crude comments in her direction as she passed. No doubt those few were the reason Boaz had instructed her to stay close to his men. The fact that she had clearly won the affection of the wealthy landowner and the fact that she was indeed a Moabitess did not set easy with some of the Israeli women or their fathers, who had indeed hoped their own daughters might win the affections of Boaz.

A month quickly passed, and Ruth found herself almost skipping to the field each morning eager to be in the company of Boaz. Each day he would reward her with at least one visit throughout the day, and that visit would always include a handful of olives along with a spoken invitation for her to join him at the evening meal. Ruth would politely accept, and Mary never failed to have a small basket of goods provided for Ruth to take home to Naomi, also under careful instruction from Boaz.

True to Ezra's comment on the first day of harvest, the barley field was cleared in record time. In a little more than a month, Ezra ended the day by informing them that the following workday would take them to the wheat field, now ripe and ready to be harvested. Boaz and Ezra had approached Ruth earlier in the day, pulling both her and Mary to the side.

"Walk with me," Boaz stated, though Ruth recognized it as a request and not a command. She looked around at what little was left to be done and nodded in agreement.

"Next, we will begin to harvest the wheat crop," Boaz explained, "and I would like to personally show you the field. Mary and Ezra will also accompany us," he clarified quickly. Ruth realized they would be in public the entire way, and it was not necessary for them to be accompanied. Yet, he had requested the presence of friends for her own comfort and peace of mind. In no way would he ever dream of tarnishing her reputation.

"I would like that," she answered honestly. Ruth did not miss the glares tossed her way by some of the maidens as they left the field. She knew that she would never be accepted by them and recognized that realization no longer concerned her the way it used to. Though Ezra and Mary accompanied them, the couple moved ahead still in view of Ruth and Boaz, but not in earshot of any conversations that may have been taking place. Ruth imagined they were talking of the approaching time that Ezra would speak to Mary's father and making hopeful plans of a coming wedding.

Thoughts of a wedding reminded Ruth of her friend Lydia, who she had been too busy to check on since the harvesting season had begun. Lydia's wedding was fast approaching, and Ruth made a mental note to make time soon for a visit to her friend. Boaz began their walk in comfortable silence, Ruth taking in the landscape around them and toying with her thoughts. Boaz continued to walk quietly, searching for the right words to say.

It was Ruth who slowed their pace and finally broke the silence. They had come upon a vast, but fairly empty, space of land. It was evident nothing was being intentionally grown here, but it was not terribly overgrown either. The sight puzzled Ruth.

"Does this field belong to you as well?" she asked, looking at the empty parcel of land.

"It does," he answered simply.

"But it is empty," she stated, though he recognized the questioning tone in her voice.

A woman who is eager to learn and questions what she does not understand. Be still my heart, Boaz thought to himself. He cleared his throat before he began to speak.

"That field is in a Sabbath of rest," he explained. Ruth looked at him, her face revealing her question, so he continued. "I have planted that field with barley for six years past. The law commands that the seventh year shall be a Sabbath of rest unto the land, and that we shall not sow it during that seventh year."

"To allow time for the soil to rest and replenish itself," she realized, and he smiled as understanding dawned on her.

"Exactly," he confirmed. "Ruth," he continued, "I have enjoyed your company over the past month, and I am encouraged that you have agreed to continue gleaning in my wheat field," he spoke honestly. "I do worry for your physical being however." She looked at him as they walked and saw the true concern on his face. "You work harder than my most efficient reapers," he continued. "You tarry with us after the workday is finished, and then you carry loads of grain back to your home. You must have chores there as well, and I do not forget the far journey you so recently endured as you came from Moab."

"I enjoy hard work," she answered honestly. "It keeps my mind off of things I cannot change and gives me a sense of purpose," she finished.

"You are a remarkable woman," he said plainly, suddenly stopping completely. Ruth turned to look at him.

"And, I am a Moabitess," she reminded him.

"Do not fault yourself for the land in which you were born," he spoke looking down into her eyes. "Ruth you are the kindest soul I have ever had the pleasure of meeting. I have watched you day after day and witnessed your goodness. Your love and care for Naomi reaches far beyond what is required of you, and the fact that you left your pagan gods for the One True God is more admirable than you can imagine. Where you came from means nothing; it is the way you live your life now that matters."

Ruth smiled up at him. "Thank you for your kind words," she spoke as she resumed walking, though her pace was slow. "You have lavished more kindness upon me than I ever expected to find in Bethlehem. I fear all are not in agreement with you in all you have so kindly stated, yet I find it no longer concerns me as it once did. I am accepted by Jehovah, and I have made a few good friends here who love me as I am," she laughed. "That is enough for me."

"Yes, you have. We love you for the person you are," he spoke, and Ruth turned her face from him as she felt it flame.

He said, "We love you" not "I" she quickly reminded herself. *Stop acting like a silly*

159

schoolgirl, she scolded herself. *You are a poor Moabite widow, and he a wealthy landowner who is kind to you because of familial ties to Elimelech.*

Boaz sought for something to say after sensing her discomfort at his words. *Was her reaction proof that she would never consider me a suitable husband?* he thought to himself. He let the silence linger for only a moment before he spoke again.

"You know," he began, "my mother served pagan gods before she married my father," he paused realizing his statement had captured Ruth's attention. Quickly, she stopped and turned to face him once again. He nodded and reached for the scarlet fabric at his waist. Ruth had noticed the fabric before, but assumed it was some sort of custom she was unfamiliar with which had something to do with his status as the owner of the field. He pulled the garment free and held it out to her. She took it almost reverently, caressing the material gently between her fingers.

Time had taken its toll on the piece, but it was still a breathtaking garment. The color, now slightly faded in spots, could still be detected in some areas as a rich, deep, scarlet color such as Ruth had never seen. Flecks of gold had been woven carefully and intricately into the material and caught the sunlight in such a way that the piece seemed to dance and glisten before her eyes.

"It is beautiful," she said in admiration. "I have never seen anything like it," she spoke honestly, gently handing the piece back to its owner. Boaz took the garment back from her and looked at it with so much love and appreciation that Ruth thought he may weep.

"This was my mother's," he began. "She wove it from flax that she had planted herself, dyed it to the color of her liking herself, used it to help my father escape her town, and then used it to guide him back to her home where he would return and usher her to safety," he stated as he attached the piece again to his belt.

"That sounds like a very interesting story," Rahab laughed urging him to tell her more. "Please continue," she requested.

Thankful for a subject that intrigued her, Boaz gently took Ruth's arm and rested it in his resuming their stroll. "My mother was a harlot," he admitted slowly, "in the town of Jericho."

"Jericho!" Ruth interrupted, excitement filling her. "I saw the remnants as Naomi and I crossed the Jordan River!"

"Yes, you did," he continued, surprised the name of the town had caught her attention over his admission that his mother had been a harlot. "So, I assume you know the story of Jericho and how the walls came down in that great city." She nodded but kept quiet, eager for him to continue. They walked slowly her eyes never leaving his face as he talked.

"My mother lived among the outer walls of the town, and had her "business" there. My father was an Israelite who had been wandering the desert for years, literally his entire life, in search of the land promised to our people by Jehovah. He was born during the wanderings and grew up in the desert they searched. My mother had visited her family one day, on the outskirts of the city, and was returning to her home when she met my father for the first time. He actually rescued her from a man outside the city gates. I believe my father was smitten with her from the beginning, for he confessed to me that from that time on he never closed his eyes without seeing her face."

"So, if he met your mother outside the city how does the scarlet wrap play into the story?" Ruth asked, clearly fascinated.

Boaz continued. "My father saved her from abuse at the man's hand, and then she returned to her home. Shortly after, my father along with a fellow soldier, Garret I believe was his name, had left the Israeli camp under the direction of their leader Joshua, to spy on the city of Jericho in an attempt to determine how they may conquer it. While there, some of the centurions came to expect that Israeli spies were among them in the city. In short, my mother hid my father and Garret under the large stalks of flax she was drying on her rooftop. When the centurions looked for them at her establishment, they were nowhere to be found."

"But the scarlet wrap," Ruth asked again, hanging on every word Boaz spoke.

He enjoyed having her attention so intently. "My father and Garett escaped Jericho that night by a scarlet cord," he patted the wrap wound at his waist, "which my mother had fashioned and dropped from her window. As they left, my father promised my mother safety for her assistance and instructed her to leave the cord hanging from her window until the time in which the city was conquered. Every Israeli soldier knew no harm was to come to any taking shelter in the room from where the scarlet cord was hung."

"But if the walls fell…" Ruth began, but let the question hang.

"Ah, the walls did fall," Boaz smiled as he stopped their walk once again. "All but the wall in which my mother resided. Do you remember when you saw the remnants of Jericho that one wall stood completely erect and seemingly unscathed among all the others of the city?"

"I do remember!" Ruth exclaimed as she thought about all she had seen. "And I remember thinking how interesting it was that one wall stood so tall while all the others were literally crumbled about it."

Boaz smiled. "Jehovah kept his promise, and He helped my father to keep his. When the walls fell, my mother remained safe inside the room where the scarlet cord hung. After he rescued my mother and her family, my father returned to my mother's residence and retrieved the cord. He brought it back to camp and returned it to my mother, who fashioned it into this wrap which she wore when they wed." Boaz looked down at the wrap still at his waist. "Many nights she would tuck me in with this wrap as my pillow," he spoke gently. "I keep it with me most of the time. I feel as if she is still with me when I have it."

"Come on slow pokes!" Ezra yelled playfully from ahead, breaking the trance Ruth had found herself in. He had Mary had made it to the wheat field. Boaz waved in his direction as he and Ruth slightly quickened their pace.

"My mother forsook her pagan gods, and the life she had led, and fled her land, just as you have, Ruth. In so many ways your story reminds me of my mother's. Circumstances may be different, but the outcome has been the same. Two very special women, brought up in less than perfect ways, were told of Jehovah by men who God sent to them to love them, and to tell them of Him," he said as they began to approach the wheat field. He stopped once again and turned her to face him. "Do not ever feel inadequate because of your background. Continue to trust your future to an all-knowing God Who has nothing but your best interest in mind. He will never forsake you, Ruth. Nor will I," he promised. Ruth was silent as he reached to brush a hair from her face where it danced in the breeze. Then he turned, entering the wheat field, where he joined Ezra and Mary.

Ruth followed behind and attempted to pay attention to the business the men began to discuss. She continued to think on, however, all Boaz had told her of his mother. What a fascinating woman she must have been, for the

Lord had blessed her with a son such as Boaz. Ruth reached to touch her face, which continued to tingle where his fingers had so lightly brushed across it. His touch had been so light, that she wondered if she might have imagined it.

Chapter Fifteen

Ruth returned home once again laden with goods as she had every evening for over a month. The company, it had been decided, would take a four-day break after finishing the barley harvest before they would begin to harvest the wheat. Ruth was thankful for the break which would allow her time to rest and to assist Naomi in preserving all she had accumulated, as well as time for a visit to Lydia, as she had promised herself. The break applied to all those in the employment of Boaz, and she appreciated that he cared so much for their well-being, even during his most profitable time. However, this break would also interrupt her daily visits from Boaz, and that put a bit of a damper on her spirit.

Ruth had come to enjoy the time she spent with him, both in and out of the fields. She smiled as she thought of the occasions he had come to her requesting that she "walk with him." He always had a reason; something he needed to show her perhaps or to teach her something she needed to know about the customs of life in Bethlehem. She enjoyed their time together, though she would admit that fact to no one.

What she enjoyed most about her time spent with him was the knowledge he would so eagerly share about Jehovah. She still had so much to learn, and she was eager to get to know the one true God, Whom she now served, even more. She felt there was not a question she could not take to Boaz, and if he did not have an immediate answer, he would be honest about it, search the scriptures, spend time in prayer, and then come back to her with his thoughts on the matter. She appreciated his devotion to Jehovah, and she appreciated his honesty with her.

She also enjoyed the stories he told her of his family. Boaz had indeed inherited well, but his consistent work ethic and wise business decisions had added to his wealth immensely. Ruth was proud for him, and she was proud that along with his wealth, he had maintained a kind and gentle spirit, traits which normally did not go hand in hand.

Perhaps, she thought to herself as she lay on her cot on the first morning of the break, the time away from Boaz would do her good. She should not allow herself to become so infatuated with him. Regardless of the attention he had given her, or the fact that he seemed to care not that she was a Moabitess, she still felt his kindness and generosity stemmed from his fondness for Elimelech and because Boaz himself was such a genuine human being.

How would people view him were he to take a Moabitess widow to wife? It would surely do nothing to profit his business, there were still those who had problems with her just being in Bethlehem. Presently, most people paid his kindness to her no mind, because everyone else had adored Elimelech as well, and knew that Boaz with his kind and gentle spirit would honor the man's memory and care for his widowed wife and family as much as society would allow.

Ruth rolled over on her cot and stared at the ceiling above her. She also knew that once the wheat harvest was over that there would be no cause for her to see him each day. She and Naomi would have more than enough goods to carry them through the winter, Boaz had seen to that. Once the wheat harvest ended, besides a possible encounter in town, so would her connection to Boaz.

While in the field, when Boaz was not present, Ruth had also noticed several of the young, male reapers watching her attentively. She knew by the smiles they tossed her way and from the looks in their eyes, that if their boss was agreeable to befriending a Moabite, they were compliant to it as well. They had adhered to Boaz's instructions that she was not to be touched, but she realized that any indication she gave them that she welcomed their attention was all that would be needed for them to approach her.

"There will never be another Mahlon," Ruth spoke softly, her mind going to her former husband. *But there could be a Boaz*, she thought to herself. Ruth rubbed her face with her hands and sat upright on her cot. She had to stop this. She was making herself miserable, and she had far too much to be thankful for to allow her mind to wonder on such foolish inclinations.

"Ruth, are you awake," Naomi called from the main area.

"I am coming," she responded as cheerfully as she could. Naomi could not know what absurd thoughts had been playing on her mind this morning. She would declare that Ruth had taken leave of her senses, and Naomi would feel as if she had forgotten Mahlon. That was something Ruth knew would never happen.

Ruth dressed herself and moved quickly to the main area where Naomi had prepared delicious bowls of porridge and small cakes of bread. "This looks wonderful!" Ruth exclaimed. "Why the feast," she laughed as Naomi added bowls of figs to the table.

"I am looking forward to some time with you, dear daughter," she admitted. "I have missed my companion as of late," she smiled, patting her hand.

"And we have much to do," Ruth acknowledged. "Boaz has been so generous. We must preserve all we have been given and allow not a morsel to go to waste."

Ruth bowed her head and prayed aloud for blessings on the food they were about to partake of and thanked Jehovah for his provisions. She also thanked him for Boaz and for the generosity he had shown them. Naomi could not help but smile as Ruth continued in her prayer of gratitude and appreciation, though Ruth knew nothing of Naomi's enthusiasm over her prayer.

"The majority of the barley can go to the storehouse just behind us," Naomi began. "I have cleaned there and made sure it is ready to hold all that we have need of. I have also brought jars and vessels from the barn and prepared them for use, here inside our home," she finished as she began to eat.

"If it suits you, I would like to take some bread and a jar of our grain to Lydia and her family, as a thank you for all their help when we first arrived," Ruth continued. "Lydia's wedding will be happening soon, and I am certain they could benefit from our sharing with them." She paused for Naomi's thoughts as she continued to eat.

"That is a fine idea," Naomi agreed. "I can never repay Jedidiah and Abigail for all they did, and have continued to do, since we arrived in Bethlehem. They have shared so much of their food and their time with us, and I do so enjoy Abigail's company," she admitted.

The ladies made a plan, and Ruth rose to clear the table.

"Before we begin," Naomi stopped her, "we have some catching up to do as well." She motioned for Ruth resume her seat at the table.

Ruth did as Naomi suggested and looked at her mother-in-law with a quizzical expression.

"Alright," she said slowly, her tone questioning where this was going, and afraid of where it might be, at the same time.

"Ruth, you come home each day with more grain than any gleaner has ever gleaned from any field," Naomi began.

"Boaz has been very kind to us," Ruth acknowledged.

"He has, but it is also because you are an extremely hard worker. I have not pressed you, Ruth, but pray tell me, are you happy gleaning there? Aside from Boaz, are you being treated fairly by the others?" Ruth inwardly sighed, thankful that this conversation was not going to be about any feelings she may or may not hold regarding Boaz, but about her own well-being, comfort and contentment.

Ruth reached for her mother-in-law's hand. Naomi obliged.

"I am quite content," she spoke honestly. "I will not speak untruthfully and deny that there are not some who would rather I not be in that field, but the majority of the workers there are kind and decent. I have made a good friend in both Mary and Ezra, and true to his word, Boaz keeps a very watchful eye over my well-being," she concluded.

Naomi nodded her head in agreement. Though Ruth was not aware of it, she had told her exactly what she wanted to know, that Boaz continued to be attentive of her needs and aware of her presence. Naomi smiled. Ruth took it as confirmation that her mother-in-law was satisfied with the answer she had received. Ruth stood and began to clear the table, this time, Naomi allowing her to do so.

As the older woman stood to assist her, she could not help but retain her smile. Her plan of patience was working. Naomi's declaration that Boaz was their next kinsmen had made no sense to Ruth on the day she spoke of meeting Boaz, and Ruth seemed to have all but forgotten it. Naomi had no doubt she could have reminded Boaz of this fact, and that he would have wed Ruth out of obligation on the spot, but she wanted more for her daughter-in-law. She wanted her to find, and to receive, love once again. Ruth deserved so much after all she had been through, retaining her goodness and grace through it all, and she had so much love to give.

Boaz was falling for Ruth, of this Naomi was certain. She wanted nothing more than for Boaz to wed Ruth out of love instead of obligation and to give her the life she so deserved. A life filled with peace and happiness. Even if that meant that she, Naomi, would lose the most precious person in her world as well as the only source of livelihood that she had. Jehovah had brought her this far; He would not leave her empty. But oh, how she would miss her precious Ruth, she thought, watching the younger woman busy at work.

Naomi would not reveal her plan just now, she would wait a bit longer and seek Jehovah's guidance in the meantime. He would reveal to her when the time was right, and she would explain everything to Ruth at that time.

The ladies finished their daily chores, and early that evening, Naomi encouraged Ruth to take some time to rest. She had been going almost non-stop for a month. Ruth was reluctant, but at Naomi's constant insistence, she retreated back to her room for "just a few minutes" and stretched across her cot. It did feel good to relax her aching bones, she smiled. She did not allow her mind to wander as it had been that morning, but instead began to count her blessings and before she knew it, she had fallen into a deep and peaceful sleep.

Naomi found her there over an hour later. She pulled a blanket gently over her body. Ruth never stirred, even when the old lady bent and kissed her cheek. Ruth slept soundly the remainder of the day, and into the night, for ten solid hours.

The next day the women began the task of storing their grain. Ruth laughed as she made trip after trip to their storehouse, with as much as she could possibly carry each time. "Do not forget we shall have wheat to add to the barley," she reminded Naomi as they completed the task.

Ruth removed her apron brushing dust from the grain from her head covering and tunic underneath. Naomi took in the condition of her garment, now becoming thin after her journey across the desert and through the river, in addition to all her work in the fields. A rather sobering thought occurred to Naomi. They needed money as well as food. She spoke as much to Ruth at their meal that evening.

"We will need to go into town soon, to gather supplies. You are going to need a new garment soon," she stated reaching out and touching Ruth's worn tunic.

"I do not care about that," Ruth denied, "there is still plenty of wear in this old thing," she laughed. "A little mending is needed perhaps," she admitted," noticing a small spot that had become threadbare, "but I do not believe a new garment will be in order."

"Boaz has more than provided for our nourishment, but...," Naomi began as Ruth interrupted her.

"And Jehovah will provide any other need we may have," Ruth finished closing the subject and patting the old woman's hand. "Tomorrow, I would like to take some barley to Lydia and visit for a while. Will you accompany me?" she asked.

"I will," Naomi agreed. "And I will bake an extra cake of bread to take as well," she finished, "maybe two!" The ladies shared laughter and finished their meal, enjoyed pleasant conversation, then retired to their individual rooms early that evening.

Ruth spent time thanking God for His provisions and praying that she would remain content with her lot. Naomi spent time thanking God for how far He had brought her and for the patience to wait on His timing regarding the relationship between Ruth and Boaz.

The next morning dawned bright and clear, and Naomi rose early to bake bread for their friends just as she had promised Ruth that she would. Around mid-day, the ladies poured a heaping portion of their barley into a vessel and began the short walk to the home of Jedidiah, excited about having items that, this time, they were able to share with his family. They were welcomed as soon as they arrived. Lydia embraced Ruth fiercely eager to tell her of all her upcoming plans and to hear how Ruth had fared in her gleaning.

Jedidiah took his leave to his barn soon after their arrival, giving the ladies time to visit. Abigail and Naomi settled themselves in the kitchen, and Lydia suggested to Ruth that they walk to the stream that ran just a short distance behind their home. As soon as the younger women had taken their leave, Abigail recognized that Naomi was about to bust with excitement.

"Do tell me, Naomi," Abigail chided her. "I sense an eagerness in you I have never seen before," she laughed.

"I must confess, it will be good to tell someone of the secrets I have been holding fast to this past month," she breathed. Naomi covered her mouth with her hands. Dare she confess aloud all she had been thinking? She knew that Abigail would be the soul of discretion when it came to keeping her plan in the strictest of confidence. Sensing her hesitation, but also her need of release, Abigail promised Naomi she would utter

176

not a word to anyone, not even to Jedidiah, she laughed.

With a glance outside the window to assure herself that the young women had gone, Naomi took a deep breath and began revealing her plan.

"Jehovah has been so very good to me, Abigail" she began, "and His mercies continue to this very day," she stood and began pacing in front of her friend, unable to be still in her excitement. "Ruth came to me a little over a month ago requesting that she be allowed to glean."

"And it appears she has done very well," Abigail acknowledged.

"You have no idea," Naomi agreed nodding her head. "By the grace of Jehovah, Ruth ended up in the field of Boaz. I had forgotten the man even existed!" Naomi quieted herself realizing she had raised her voice in her excitement.

Abigail stared blankly at her friend, a puzzled expression on her face. "Alright…" Abigail said slowly, clearly not understanding why this was such a revelation. "Boaz lives…and…" her voice trailed off as she shrugged her shoulders in confusion.

Naomi moved a chair to face Abigail. "Let me back up," she insisted calming herself with another deep breath and taking the seat directly across from her dearest friend. "Elimelech's direct relatives were among the Israeli wanderers of the desert who searched for the Promised Land for forty years," she began. "You see Elimelech, and one younger brother, were born very late in life to their mother and father. His older brother, Nahshon, was quite the adventurer and had left home when Elimelech was still quite young. He adored his older brother Nahshon and was quite upset when he left them, though he promised Elimelech that he would return as soon as the fortune he sought had been made.

Nahshon went to Egypt as a strong young man but was unfortunately enslaved there. Once Moses freed our people, Nahshon was already an old man, though still not too old to marry, and during the early part of those forty years, a son was born to him. Sadly, Nahshon died as they continued their wandering in the wilderness. He never saw the Promised Land and obviously never returned home, but his son, Salmon rose to be a prince among the people. Salmon had promised his father on his deathbed that he would find Elimelech and tell him of all that had transpired and why Nahshon's promise to Elimelech to return home had not been kept.

Salmon had a mighty part in the defeat of Jericho, and in the process of conquering that city, he met and eventually wed a woman he rescued from there. It was quite a beautiful story, and the two were happy for many, many years. They had a child, Abigail," Naomi spoke slowly as she stared into the face of her friend. "Boaz is their son."

Abigail stared at her dearest friend in jaw-dropping surprise. "Naomi," she began joining hands with the older woman as they both rose to their feet "this means that Boaz…" her voice trailed off unable to verbalize what she had learned.

"Yes!" Naomi cried as she finished the sentence for Abigail, "Boaz is our next kinsman!" The ladies embraced in a fit of laughter and tears.

"Blessed be, Jehovah!" Abigail exclaimed as she broke their embrace, "but Naomi why," she asked wiping tears of joy from her eyes and lowering her voice, "why keep this such a secret? You know the integrity of Boaz; he would wed Ruth on the spot!"

"Out of obligation," Naomi agreed quieting her friend. "I want more for them both, and through Jehovah's goodness, Boaz is developing an affection for Ruth, and I dare say, she is developing an affection for him. I will tell her," she promised, "as soon as Jehovah gives me leave to do so, but for now, I must have patience and your promise once again of discretion."

"I promise, my precious friend" Abigail vowed hugging Naomi tightly once more. "I will not utter a word!"

"Does Boaz know?" Abigail asked finally.

Naomi considered the question that had not even occurred to her.

"I am not sure," she answered honestly. "Salmon kept his promise to his father and found

Elimelech, visiting our home often before we left for Moab. He even brought his wife and son on occasion, but Boaz would have been very young. I do not know if he remembers the kinship or not," she spoke truthfully.

"Regardless, he will know eventually," Abigail stated. "When the time is right."

"Yes," Naomi agreed. "But by then, I pray that his kinship to us does not even matter."

Chapter Sixteen

Lydia shared her plans with Ruth as they walked. Ruth loved seeing her friend so eager and so excited about beginning her life with Samuel. It reminded her of when Mahlon had asked for her hand. *Will I ever be that happy again?* she wondered quietly to herself. Samuel had worked hard to ensure a nice beginning for himself and Lydia. They would live in close proximity to both their parents, and Ruth was pleased to find out, close to her and Naomi as well. Though their stroll was leisurely, it did not take very long for them to reach the stream.

"Listen to me prattle on, monopolizing the conversation," Lydia apologized. "Tell me, Ruth, how have you been? How did your gleaning go?" she asked.

"There is no need of an apology!" Ruth laughed at her friend. "I have so enjoyed hearing your plans." She paused before continuing, but Lydia's expression was clear that she intended for her to. "Well…" Ruth began "it has been interesting," she admitted.

"How so?" Lydia egged her on taking her by the arm and directing her slowly back toward the house.

"Remember when you told me to allow Jehovah to direct me to the field where I was to glean?" Ruth asked.

"Yes…" Lydia acknowledged, rolling her hands for Ruth to continue.

"Well, He did. I ended up in a field belonging to Boaz, and you will never believe who is overseeing that field," she continued. "Ezra!"

Lydia gasped in delight. "Wonderful! Then you were able to glean freely, and you did well?" Lydia asked.

Ruth relayed all the happenings of the past month to Lydia. She left out almost nothing. She told her of her new friend, Mary. She told her of the generous way in which Boaz treated her, she told her of the meals she had been invited to, that she had been allowed to glean among the sheaves, and of the lavish amount of barley that she had brought home each day. She also told her that Boaz had asked her to return to glean wheat from his field as well.

Lydia listened intently, soaking in everything Ruth was telling her before she finally spoke again. They had neared the house by that point, so Lydia pulled Ruth behind the barn. They settled on a large rock big enough to seat them both comfortably.

"Ruth," Lydia began sincerely, "Do you love him?" she asked, looking Ruth squarely in the face.

"Love who?" Ruth scoffed, waving her friend's suggestion aside.

"I do not jest," Lydia chuckled at her reaction to the question. "Do you love, Boaz?" Ruth was quiet. She had not told a lie since she had come to know Jehovah as the one true God. She looked at her friend and searched her face. She honestly was not sure how to answer the question.

"I do not know," she finally answered honestly. "I loved Mahlon," she continued. "He was so easy to love, and I was so new to the idea of what love is all about. And I sincerely appreciate all that Boaz has done for me, but I feel he has done so out of respect for Elimelech's memory. I feel he would have done the same for you had you been in the situation I am in. I am afraid to lose my heart to him, Lydia. It has been broken so severely already. I do not think I could bare to have it broken again."

Lydia looked at her friend, her honesty causing tears to fill her eyes. "I do not pretend to know all you have gone through, Ruth," she admitted, "but I do know that Jehovah does not make mistakes and that nothing happens without a reason. It is clearly He who led you to that field. It is clearly He who allowed Boaz to notice and inquire about you. If Jehovah has a future for you with Boaz, do not let fear stand in your way, and if He does not, be simply thankful for all that He has provided through Boaz thus far."

Ruth was amazed at the wisdom of her friend. She hugged her and thanked her, then asked her to keep their conversation between the two of them. She would never want Naomi to feel she was disrespecting Mahlon's memory by considering a future with someone else. Lydia promised, and the two moved back indoors to end their visit with some time with the older ladies.

Once they were all back together, Lydia and Abigail excused themselves and returned with a large satchel.

"I do not want to insult you with our offer, but I believe we are close enough friends that pride will not be an issue," Abigail began. Ruth and Naomi looked at one another and shook their heads, affirming her statement. "We have finished Lydia's trousseau for her upcoming marriage, and we have a bit of material left," Abigail began.

"It is not a lot, but it is enough for one garment, maybe even two. I would like for you to have it, Ruth," Lydia smiled, handing the satchel of material to her friend.

Ruth laughed as she accepted the bag. "You are too kind, both of you," she smiled.

Naomi was almost speechless. "Just this morning, I was addressing the fact that Ruth would need a new garment soon," Naomi sighed. "Now this," she stated, shaking her head in amazement, moving to hug her friend.

"How can we ever repay you, Abigail?" Naomi asked, continuing to embrace her dearest friend.

"Your friendship is payment enough, Naomi," she said aloud. Then for Naomi's ears alone, "Ask me again if your plan works, and Ruth weds a certain wealthy landowner," she laughed, winking at the older woman as they broke the embrace. Both ladies laughed together.

They took their leave with more hugs and promised to visit again soon, next time at the home of Naomi and Ruth. With promises and well-wishes, the ladies enjoyed their short walk home, both talking of the wonderful visit but neither of them revealing their "secret" conversations to the other. They did talk about how wonderful it felt to laugh again and be out from under the cloud of misery they had experienced during their time in Moab. They were thankful, though some memories were still painful, that those days were behind them and that now they could focus on their future.

As they neared their home, Ruth paused at the sight of a small leather satchel hanging from the doorpost.

"What is this," she asked of Naomi who shrugged her shoulders in confusion. Taking the satchel from the door post, the ladies moved inside the house. Once inside, they placed the satchel on the table and began to remove the contents. A cake of bread, a cruz of oil, and a small vessel containing parched corn, as well as another smaller pouch was tucked inside.

"There is no note, no indication of who could have left this for us?" Naomi questioned looking over the contents. Ruth's heart thundered in her chest. She held the smaller pouch in her hand, opening it slowly. Once she saw the contents it held, she knew exactly who had left this for them. Naomi watched her face light up as Ruth carefully turned the pouch upside down and a small handful of olives escaped from inside.

"I know exactly who this is from," she laughed. Naomi framed Ruth's face and gently kissed her cheek. No words were needed as the old woman turned away allowing Ruth her moment. She wanted to tell Ruth everything, she wanted to declare it was time, but Jehovah said, "Wait," so wait she did.

On her final day of the break, Naomi and Ruth decided to head into town. Ruth carried the last of the coins they had from the items they had sold in Moab in a small satchel by her waist. Due to the fabric Lydia and Abigail had given them, new garments would not be an issue, but a sewing needle, some thread, and a few other supplies would be. Those things, along with some lentils, could easily be purchased in town.

The streets were full of vendors as they were almost every day. Ruth was much more familiar and felt much more comfortable today than she had on her first visit to town. The ladies purchased all they came for and were about to make their way back home when a voice calling their names caught their attention.

"Ruth!" the voice called. "Naomi!" the ladies stopped, turning about to see who was calling to them. A young lad came running toward them, a small satchel in his hand. Excited to have caught up to them, he held the satchel out to Ruth.

"What is this," she asked, patting the young lad on his head.

"I was sent to fetch this to you," he explained. "It was purchased on your behalf, and I was told to give it to you the next time you and Naomi were in town."

Ruth took the satchel from him and looked inside. She chuckled when she saw the remnants. Naomi looked from Ruth to the lad and back again.

"Who purchased these," Ruth laughed, directing her question to the boy.

"I was told not to tell!" he informed her, "and was given a whole shekel to keep quiet!" he proudly announced.

"Well, when you see this mystery person again, please thank him for me," she spoke, patting the boy on the head dismissing him.

"I will," he promised and then bounded away as quickly as he came.

Naomi loved the way Ruth was smiling as she peeked inside the satchel again.

"Might that be olives?" Naomi asked with a side glance and a smile at her daughter-in-law.

Ruth looked at the woman beside her as they resumed their pace.

"It might be," she affirmed shyly with a grin.

Ruth was up early the next morning, ready to return to work and to the fields where she was hopeful of seeing Boaz. She had enjoyed her time off with Naomi, but she was eager to work again. One thing her mother had taught her in Moab was that being idle was not good for one's disposition. She thought of her parents often and wondered if she had stayed in Moab could she have ever convinced them to forsake their pagan gods as she had and to trust in Jehovah? She had no doubt she was where she was supposed to be now, but she did think of those she had left behind often.

She wondered about Orpah and if she continued on in her state of depression or if she had moved on once she had returned to Moab without her in-laws. Ruth pulled a brush through her long dark hair as she pondered on these things, then covered it with her worn vail.

She left home a little earlier, knowing the wheat field was a short distance farther than the barley field had been. She did not mind. It gave her time to think. Though she still felt that Boaz's kindness stemmed from a relationship he had shared with Elimelech, she could not figure out if that was still his only reason for being kind to her. The olives for instance. Why did he continue bestowing her favorite fruit upon her if he was only being kind for the sake of Elimelech? It was not necessary. And his constant effort to seek her out and talk with her, that was more than simple kindness, was it not?

Ruth continued thinking on these things. She arrived at the wheat field at the same time many others were approaching. She saw many familiar faces, but was also met with some new ones. Mary was in the distance, and Ruth crossed quickly to her. She greeted her friend with a smile. Mary returned the greeting, then pulled Ruth quickly to the side.

"Be weary," she warned.

"Of?" Ruth questioned.

"Both Nabal's oldest son and daughter have come to glean." Mary tossed her head in the direction of the pair. "Ezra told me of your encounter with Nabal. He cannot run them off unless they cause a scene, and he does not want to bring you to their attention if they do not know who you are. They may not even know about their father's encounter with you in the marketplace when you first came to Bethlehem. Ezra has no concern over the daughter, she is too young to do you physical harm, but no doubt they share the same twisted views of their fool father," she spat, "so stay close to Ezra."

"Where is Boaz?" Ruth questioned looking around the field. Mary smiled.

"He had to go out of town on business," she shrugged, "but he left this for you," she stated extending a small leather satchel. Ruth laughed, taking the bag from her friend. She shook her head at the handful of olives within.

"I have never seen him like this, Ruth," Mary admitted. "And I do not suspect I ever will again."

"I am a Moabitess widow…" she began, but Mary quickly interrupted her.

"And he does not seem to care," Mary finished.

Ruth changed the subject. "This field does not look nearly as large as the barley field we cleared."

"It is not. We will finish this field in no time," she acknowledged. "The same rules apply here as in the barley field. Boaz said you are to glean among our sheaves just as you did there," she smiled.

Ruth thanked her and went to work. She put in a full day and was invited by Ezra to join them for the evening meal. She accepted, and felt comfortable, though a little lonely that Boaz was not in attendance. She hoped he would be back on the morrow, and she did not hide her pleasure when he was.

Chapter Seventeen

"Happy morning," Boaz smiled, as Ruth approached the field the next day. He seemed to be awaiting her arrival there.

"Happy morning," she returned with a smile.

"What do you think of our wheat?" he asked looking across the field. Much progress had been made the day before.

"It is the finest wheat I have ever had the pleasure of gleaning," she spoke honestly.

"And how much wheat have you gleaned?" he asked curiously.

"This is the first," she admitted with a smile causing him to laugh out loud. She loved the sound of his laughter but blushed when the sound caught the attention of so many others.

"Thank you for all the olives," she stated shyly, her face continuing to color slightly. Boaz secretly loved the few times he had caused her face to flush. He must look for ways to do so more often.

"You are welcome," he stated. "There are plenty more to come, I promise you." He gently lifted her hand, kissing it gently. "Have a most pleasant day and join us for our evening meal," he requested.

Ruth simply smiled and bowed her head in acceptance of the invitation.

The sun was high and the work was hard, but Ruth truly enjoyed it. She stayed close to Ezra per instructions from Mary, especially when she noticed Nabal's son, whom Mary had pointed out to her, watching her so intently. She worked through the day, enjoyed the evening meal with Boaz and his people per his request, and returned home each evening bearing loads of wheat and other goods the same as when they had harvested the barley.

Ruth could not deny the fact, however, that each day brought a little sadness knowing that the gathering of the wheat was almost complete. Completion of the crop would end her time in the fields with Boaz and her new friends. Mary had told her just this morning that in a little less than a week, the field would be completely harvested. The past two months had brought more joy to her life than Ruth had felt since Mahlon had passed. It ached her very soul that it was all about to come to an end, though Mary brimmed with excitement that once the harvest was finished, Ezra would ask her father for her hand.

With a prayer for contentment, Ruth continued her work. She was intent on her task this morning, not realizing how isolated she had become from the rest of the group, until she heard a voice she had not heard before.

"So, you are Ruth," the voice stated slowly, dripping with revulsion. She turned quickly to see Nabal's son speaking to her. He had come upon her from behind, and she had not heard him approach. She dropped her head, the smirk on his face disgusting her.

"I am," she acknowledged. She moved to get past him, but he blocked her way.

"My father says you are a Moabite. I have not spoken to a Moabite before," he continued. He reached out to pluck a piece of straw from Ruth's basket and began to chew it between his teeth.

"Well, now you can add that to your list of accomplishments," she answered, her face solemn. "If you will excuse me," she began politely, and again he blocked her path.

"Why are you in such a hurry?" he asked continuing to chew on the straw between his teeth. "You are a pretty little thing. For a Moabitess," he smirked moving closer to her. "I thought I might get to know you a little better since the boss does not have you tied up at the moment."

"That is not a good idea," she spoke sternly. He laughed, and the sound made Ruth's stomach turn. Alarm coursed through her body as he reached out to grasp her. She ducked, and he missed her arm but caught her tunic, causing herself and her basket of wheat to fall to the ground.

"Now look at what you've done, Moabite," he seethed. "You went and spilled your basket," he held her body to the ground with his foot. "You sure are pretty to be a Moabite," he repeated as Ruth attempted to get up. He reached down, holding fast to her tunic, pinning her to the ground. She struggled and was about to scream when his hand went over her mouth. "Just hush your pretty little mouth," he warned. "There is not a soul in all of Bethlehem Judea who would take a Moabite's word over mine!" he promised with a horrifying grin.

Ruth lifted her knee and kicked him hard. He fell back with a howl and a thud at the same time as two massive hands lifted him straight from the ground. Ruth watched as his head jerked one way and then the next, the fists which had grabbed him, punching his face once and then again before literally throwing his body from the field.

"DO NOT EVER COME NEAR HER OR ANY OF MY PROPERTIES AGAIN!" Boaz thundered plainly. Ruth had never heard him speak in that tone before and hoped she never had cause to again. Though thankful for it, it sent shivers up her spine.

The boy lay on the ground outside the perimeters of the field, writhing in pain. Ruth had gotten to her knees and was beginning to stand when Boaz rushed to her side. He knelt before her, framing her face with his hands, his knuckles bloody from the punches he had just inflicted on the boy. Frantically, he searched her face for signs of injury.

"Did he hurt you? Are you alright?" He launched question after question about her well-being at her so quickly that she could not answer verbally, she could only shake her head "no" that she had not been hurt. Without thought he pulled her to himself cradling her against his chest. His embrace was fierce, yet gentle, and he held her until her breathing slowed.

Ezra had reached the scene now, hearing the commotion, and worked to pull the boy to his feet before kicking him again.

"You heard Boaz," he instructed. "Get off this property, and do not ever let me catch you near us again," he seethed through clenched teeth. The boy stumbled away as quickly as he could, and Ezra joined Ruth and Boaz. Boaz released his embrace as Ruth began to pull away, but did not take his hands from her arms. He calmed himself before speaking again, more gently this time. He could feel her body continuing to tremble.

"Ruth, are you alright?" he asked again.

"I am," she answered this time, though her voice was barely above a whisper. "Thank you for your assistance." She was so embarrassed at what had happened. She pulled away from him and began to quickly pull the stalks of wheat back toward herself, adding them back to her basket.

"I am so sorry," she began, "to have caused you trouble…." she attempted, but her voice broke as a sob caught in her throat. Boaz pulled her to her feet and held her in his arms as she cried. Fortunately for Ruth, they were still alone, and no one else, besides Ezra, knew of what had happened. That man stood by, not knowing exactly what course of action to take. Did he leave? Did he stay? He continued to stand fast when his employer caught his eye.

"Ruth, you have caused me anything but problems," Boaz spoke as she cried. He held her close until her sobs abated. "Do not ever utter such an apology again," he instructed her. She calmed herself and took a deep breath, once more pulling from his embrace. No man had ever held her as she cried. Not even Mahlon.

"I will take my leave," she began, wiping her face with her tunic, but he held up his hand, stopping her from speaking.

"You will not," he began. "You will collect yourself, and you will join me for the evening meal as you promised. Our harvest is finished, so the meal tonight may run a bit longer. It will be later than usual, so I will personally escort you home." He was assertive but not menacing. Ruth knew that even at his pointed remarks, this was still a request and not a command. His voice softened as he looked into her face. "If you will allow me to," he finished kindly with a smile.

Ruth nodded her head and allowed him to take her arm, placing it inside his own. "No one is to hear of this, Ezra," he commanded to the man behind them.

"Yes, Sir," Ezra agreed as he fell in step behind Boaz and Ruth.

"But your hands," Ruth asked rubbing across his broken knuckles, then using her tunic to gently wipe them.

Boaz looked at his bloody fists, "A pathetic hog wandered into the field. I cannot allow such filth to mar my produce," he jested. She smiled up at him. "Well, it is not a complete lie," he justified.

The pair made their way to the tent where the meal had been prepared. Ruth ate her fill, and Mary packed Naomi a small bag, but this evening, true to his word, Boaz escorted Ruth home.

They were quiet as they walked, and for the first time, they were unaccompanied. Boaz carried her earnings of the day, and Ruth carried the bag of goods for Naomi, as well as a small sack of olives Boaz had given her.

"Thank you again," she spoke as they walked. "For everything," she concluded. "I can honestly say that I have enjoyed my time in your fields," she paused, "save today," she spoke truthfully.

"And I have thoroughly enjoyed you being there," he commented, "even today," he smiled to her.

"I am sorry about your hands," she continued looking at his red and swollen knuckles. The bleeding had stopped, but they were quite bruised. She wondered of the boy's face, then realized she did not care.

"Do they hurt much?" she asked, her finger rubbing softly across them.

"They will heal," he stated simply. He cared not for the state of his hands, only for the well-being of the woman beside of him. "I must say you were doing a fine job holding your own," he teased.

"You could not be soft in Moab. The people there are quite different," she finished.

"Were you ever harmed in Moab?" he asked genuinely curious.

"No," she answered quickly. "My father taught us to protect ourselves. That was the thing about the god, Chemosh," Ruth continued, "those who served him, and all of Moab did, could find reason for almost any of their actions. They would simply claim Chemosh had instructed them to do whatever act they had done, and it was left at that. That was one of the many things I never felt comfortable with. Men were really their own gods, they simply claimed their actions in the name of Chemosh, and everyone accepted whatever it was."

"I am sorry you grew up in such a place," he began, stopping to look at her, "and I am sorry that you lost your husband in such a way that brought you so much pain," he continued, "but I am not sorry that you are here, Ruth," he finished taking her hand in his. They had reached her door. "I remember this place," he smiled as he looked around. "My father used to bring me here," he admitted.

"You came here?" she questioned. "To see Elimelech, I presume."

"Yes, and his family," he concluded. "Actually, Ruth," he began but was interrupted when the door was opened suddenly by Naomi. He dropped her hand, and the conversation, quickly.

"I thought I heard voices outside my door," Naomi greeted him with a smile. "Boaz! It is so good to see you!" she exclaimed embracing him in a hug. "The last time I saw you, you barely reached my waist!" she laughed, "now I am barely above yours!"

"And it is good to see you, Naomi!" he stated enthusiastically. "Thank you for allowing Ruth to glean in my fields these past two months," he stated. "Her work ethic matches my own, and her beauty and disposition are matched by no other," he stated causing Ruth's face to flame.

"She is a welcome addition to my home," Naomi spoke honestly. "I would not have survived these last few years without her," she continued, "and we would not survive the winter without you," she admitted. "Thank you for the abundance of goods you have provided. We will be able to survive beyond next year's harvest with all you have bestowed upon us. Please know that you are always welcome in our home, Boaz," she finished.

"Thank you kindly, Naomi," he spoke sincerely with a slight bow. "I must take my leave now that I have seen you safely home, Ruth."

"Whatever happened to your hands?" Naomi questioned, suddenly noticing his knuckles.

"Just a pathetic, nasty hog that had wandered into my field," he answered with a wink in Ruth's direction. She chuckled and rolled her eyes, an expression he had not seen from her before but thought was absolutely adorable.

"Until we meet again," he spoke looking into her face.

"Goodbye, Boaz," she returned softly, and with a bow in her direction, he was gone.

Chapter Eighteen

Ruth did not quite know what to do with herself the next morning. She busied herself with her normal chores and assisted Naomi with the cooking. She noticed that her mother-in-law seemed unusually happy today, but she assumed it was because she was back at home and that Naomi would again have some company in her house. Ruth remained as cheerful as possible, though inside she was saddened by the fact her days in the field were over, for the time being anyway. She recounted the events of yesterday in her mind, and thought again of how she felt when Boaz had held her as she cried.

Mahlon had been a good husband, and though he was attentive to her needs, he had always left her in solitude if she was sad or hurt. He had never been the consoling type, spending the majority of his time outdoors with his brother and leaving her in the companionship of his mother. Ruth had never doubted his love for her, and before Mahlon, she had never experienced love, so she did not know things could be any different. He was a good provider, a good teacher and a good man. That was all she had ever expected him to be.

Boaz was different. Ruth had appreciated the feeling of security that Boaz had provided when he was with her, and in truth, she longed for it. His arms were strong, yet gentle, and when he had held her, she had feared nothing. He made her feel special and appreciated, and when he looked at her with such tenderness and kindness in his eyes, her heart forgot to beat. He cared for her well-being both physically and mentally, and she knew he sought her fortune and comfort above his own. The talks they shared and the time they spent together had shown her a companionship like she had never known. She shook her head to clear her thoughts and refused to continue to think on the matter.

Noon approached quickly, and Ruth noticed an unusually heavy spread for the mid-day meal. Naomi had also spent some time outside before laying the meal on the table, but Ruth respected the older woman's privacy and did not pry.

"There is a nice breeze blowing this day," Naomi smiled as she took her place across from Ruth at the table. Ruth nodded in agreement. She too had noticed the breeze, but did not understand what about it was so special. "I would like to speak with you about something rather personal," Naomi began, "and I require your complete honesty." She paused for Ruth's reaction.

"Of course, Naomi," Ruth promised, paying close attention to her mother-in-law.

"What are your feelings toward Boaz now that the harvest is complete?" she asked pointedly.

The question took Ruth completely off guard. She looked at Naomi with a bewildered expression, not sure how to answer the question and honestly afraid to. Naomi understood her reserve.

"Let me rephrase my question, dear," she began again. "Now that the harvest is complete, and you are no longer expected to gather and glean from his fields, what are your feelings regarding Boaz?" She paused again, giving Ruth time to process her thoughts.

"Naomi," Ruth began toying with a morsel of bread, "I am very fond of the kindness that Boaz has bestowed upon us. I have never met a man with a more gentle and caring spirit...." she let the sentence hang and shrugged her shoulders. "Why are you asking me this, Naomi?" she finally asked almost aggressively.

"Do you love him? Can you see yourself spending the remainder of your days with him?" Naomi finally asked.

A single tear began to roll along Ruth's face. She would not lie to this woman, though it pained her to admit the truth.

"I do not wish you to think harshly of me Naomi, and I do not wish for you to feel I have disrespected the memory of your son. But yes, I would love nothing more than to spend the rest of my time on this earth with Boaz," she admitted for the first time to anyone, including herself. She braced herself for the torrent of emotions she expected to come from her admission. What she received, though, was a torrent of love.

Naomi rose and went to her precious daughter-in-law; her smile spreading across her withered face.

"Then rise up my daughter, and do exactly as I tell you!" she exclaimed pulling Ruth from her chair.

"What?" Ruth asked clearly perplexed at the way her mother-in-law was responding to her answer.

"Ruth, do you remember the night you first came home from the fields, the night you told me that you had met Boaz?"

"Yes, of course," she said her face still filled with questions.

"Do you remember my excitement that night? I was overjoyed because in my own grief and sorrow, I had forgotten that Boaz even existed. Ruth, Boaz is one of our next kinsmen. He is allowed by our laws to marry you and redeem you from the life you now know."

"But, I am a Moabitess," Ruth reminded her.

"He does not care, my daughter, and neither do I!" she almost shouted in excitement. "Boaz would have married you on the spot out of obligation had it been asked of him, but now I am certain he will marry you out of love and adoration for the person that you are! This is the moment I have been waiting for." Ruth searched her face, her eyes full of questions.

My daughter," Naomi continued, "shall I not seek rest for thee that it may be well with thee? And now is not Boaz of our kindred, with whose maidens thou wast? Behold, he winnoweth barley to night in the threshing floor. Wash thyself therefore, and anoint thee, and put thy raiment upon thee, and get thee down to the floor!"

Ruth stared at the woman before her struggling to make sense of it all. Her feelings, the laws, it was too much. Tears began to fill her eyes.

Naomi paused, realizing she was overwhelming her daughter-in-law, who was so clearly confused by everything Naomi was throwing at her.

"Follow my instructions, Ruth. I will not mislead you," Naomi promised. "Allow me to help you find the peace, and love, and protection, that you so desperately deserve. Trust me," Naomi begged her.

Ruth nodded her head. "Whatever you say, Naomi, I will do," Ruth agreed.

"Good. Good my daughter." Naomi breathed deeply, then rushed to her room. When she came back, she brought with her a beautiful new garment she had constructed from the material given to them by Abigail and Lydia. "This is what you shall wear," Naomi smiled to her handing Ruth the garment.

"Naomi, it is beautiful," Ruth admitted as she ran the garment between her fingers. "I have never seen anything so beautiful."

"I am thrilled you think so, but it will be all the more so when you put it on," the old woman smiled to her. "Now, go wash yourself, put on the garment, and use the oils you received from your wedding to Mahlon. I will give you further instructions once you have done these things," she promised. "Go, quickly!" she instructed.

Ruth rose immediately and almost ran to her room, grabbing the wash basin as she went. Naomi laughed and uttered a prayer, petitioning Jehovah to give her exactly the right words to instruct Ruth in what was to come and for grace to let her go.

An hour passed before Ruth appeared again to Naomi, this time clean, anointed, and wearing the garment Naomi had fashioned for her. It fit her perfectly, the color accenting her eyes, just as Naomi had predicted. Her hair was brushed and left long down her back, the slightest amount of curl teasing the edges, her new veil covering it lightly. She looked breathtaking, and Naomi knew there was no way Ruth would remain a widow after this night. She took her daughter-in-law's hands and gave her clear instructions for the rest of the evening.

"Get thee down to the floor: but make not thyself known unto the man, until he shall have done eating and drinking. And it shall be, when he lieth down, that thou shalt mark the place where he shall lie, and thou shalt go in, and uncover his feet, and lay thee down; and he will tell thee what thou shalt do."

Ruth looked into this woman's eyes who had been everything to her. "All that thou sayest unto me I will do," she promised. She kissed her withered cheek, thanked her again for making her garment, and turned to go. Naomi watched her walk away, and then held her arms out as Ruth turned to her once again and fled back into a fierce embrace.

"I love you, Naomi," she spoke aloud as she held this woman who was as dear to her as any other.

"And I love you, dear daughter," she returned. Ruth broke the embrace, turned again, and vanished out of sight into the night.

Naomi closed the door once she was out of sight and leaned against it, praying for Jehovah's safety as Ruth made her way to the threshing floor and for the acceptance she deserved once she arrived there.

Ruth made her way quickly to the threshing floor, being extra careful of her garment along the way. As she arrived, she understood why Naomi had been so conscious of the breeze she had mentioned earlier. Ruth had heard of winnowing before, but she had never witnessed the process being done.

She watched Boaz from her place as he assisted with the task. He, Ezra, and several others were in the center of the room. Piles and piles of grain lay heaped around them. Time and again they would scoop the grain into large shovels, then throw it high into the air. As the breeze caught the grain in the air, the heavy grain would fall back to the ground, the breeze doing the work of separating the chaff which would blow away into the night.

Ruth made her way into the crowd that was gathered, finally finding Mary. They talked and laughed for hours as the men continued the arduous task. Ruth noticed the muscles strain in Boaz's arms as he continually tossed the grain into the air and imagined how the men's backs must ache and burn from the effort of lifting the heavy, countless shovels of grain again and again.

Finally, the winnowing was complete and the men begin to take their fill of the feast. Each time Ruth would see Boaz attempting to seek her out, Naomi's words would burn in her ears, "*But make not thyself known unto the man, until he shall have done eating and drinking.*" Time and again she would flash him a smile and move further into the crowd. Per her mother-in-law's instructions, she must keep her distance from him until the time was right.

The hard work he had endured and his full stomach took a toll on Boaz. He sought Ruth once more, did not see her, and assuming she had left, took his rest at the end of a large heap of corn. Ruth watched him from behind a beam and appreciated that he would be easy to find once the lanterns had gone out.

As the men who had been winnowing began to bed down for the night, it did not take long for the rest of the party to follow suit. Ruth lay in her place amongst the crowd until all that was heard were soft snores and gentle breathing. Carefully, and quietly, she made her way across the floor, stepping over this person and around the next until she reached the place where Boaz lay.

In the moonlight Ruth could make out his features. "*He is such a handsome man,*" she thought. He was tired and slept soundly. Ruth silently offered thanks to Jehovah for bringing her to this place and into his presence. She was not sure what would happen after this, but Naomi would never lead her down a path that she had not first petitioned Jehovah for guidance, so Ruth followed her directions exactly, just as she had promised she would. Very gently, she knelt at his feet, softly removing the covers from over them. Once his feet were uncovered, Ruth laid herself down and slept, trusting in the knowledge of Naomi and in the direction of Jehovah.

Boaz stirred, but was not sure what had awoken him. He just knew that his bones ached, and his arms burned from the tasks he had performed just a few hours before. He looked to where the moon hung in the sky. "*It must be close to midnight,*" he thought as he turned to make himself comfortable.

Suddenly he realized he was not alone in his space! Someone had joined him. Boaz sat upright in the dark, aware of a woman who slept at his now bare feet. He knew the customs of their land, but what he did not know was who was there, carrying them out.

"Who art thou," he demanded softly.

Ruth had awoken as Boaz stirred. "I am Ruth, thine handmaid," she spoke softly so only he could hear. "Spread therefore thy skirt over thine handmaid; for thou art a near kinsman."

Boaz could scarcely believe what was happening. The moment he had prayed for had come to pass. He rubbed his face and eyes to assure himself that he was not caught up in a dream. She was still there, he felt her presence at his feet. He knew now that Ruth would not only entertain a relationship with him, but that she actually desired it. He almost hated himself for the truth he was about to have to reveal to her, the reason his business had taken him away at the first of the wheat harvest. Regardless, of his burden, he could not send her away this night, and he could not send her away not knowing that he shared the same affection for her that she shared of him.

Boaz moved quietly, positioning himself directly in front of Ruth being careful not to awake the other men laying closest to him. He spoke in a whisper with all sincerity as he looked into her face by the light of the moon.

"Blessed be thou of the Lord, my daughter: for thou has shewed more kindness in the latter end than at the beginning, inasmuch as thou followedst not young men, whether poor or rich. And now, my daughter, fear not; I will do to thee all that thou requirest: for all the city of my people doth know that thou are a virtuous woman. And now it is true that I am thy near kinsman:" he paused before he continued, "howbeit there is a kinsman nearer than I."

Ruth felt as if she had been kicked in the chest. Boaz had begun by accepting her proposal. She had allowed herself to hope that she would be held by him again. She had allowed herself to hope that this man would be her husband and that she would not be alone anymore. She had allowed herself to believe that this man, who she had finally admitted that she loved would be her husband, but now Boaz had told her that someone else had rights to her before he did. Someone else. Another stranger that she could be forced to marry. She could not hide the tears that filled her eyes.

Boaz saw those tears glisten in the moonlight, and his heart broke. He moved closer still to her, careful not to frighten this precious creature before him. She remained on her knees before him. He saw the lone tear escape her eye and slide slowly along her cheek. Carefully, he framed her face with one hand, brushing the tear from her face with his thumb. He laid his forehead against hers and uttered a silent prayer.

"Please, Jehovah, if it be your will, allow me to make this woman my own," he prayed silently. Ruth did not move, cherishing his closeness, though she in fact, wanted to flee. She did not want another; she wanted Boaz. She did not want to know of another kinsman. She wanted this man to redeem her, to love her and to cherish her, and she wanted to love and cherish him for the rest of her days.

Boaz pulled his head away from hers and looked into her face once again, his hand still gently caressing her face.

"Tarry this night, and it shall be in the morning that if he will perform unto thee the part of a kinsman, well;" he paused, but knew he had no choice, "let him do the kinsman's part" he continued, "but if he will not do the part of a kinsman to thee, then will I do the part of a kinsman to thee, as the Lord liveth:"

Ruth watched intently as he moved away from her to pull a new vail from the place where he had been laying his head. He returned to her then, pushing her shoulders softly signifying for her to return to her resting place. Ruth did as he bade, Boaz tucking the veil he had purchased just that day under her head as a pillow

"Lie down until the morning," he instructed her softly. "You will be safe here, in my care" he promised. He watched as she settled herself and watched over her until sleep claimed her once again. Until then, he did not move to lie down again, for he knew he would not rest until he knew that she was once again comfortable at his feet.

Chapter Nineteen

Boaz was not sure when he drifted back to sleep, lying awake for what seemed like hours praying and petitioning Jehovah for direction, then trying to figure out for himself how to persuade the other kinsman NOT to marry Ruth. Sleep apparently claimed him eventually, however, for the sun had just begun to rise when he felt someone touch his shoulder.

He snapped awake to see Ezra pointing shockingly at Ruth, still sound asleep at his feet. With a motion for Ezra to keep quiet, Boaz moved quickly, waking her gently so as not to alarm her. Ruth stirred, raised up, and realized immediately the implications of being where she was when the others awoke. She quickly and quietly moved to another area of the threshing floor without speaking a word to Boaz or Ezra. Boaz watched her take an empty pallet near Mary, then diverted his attention to Ezra.

"Let it not be known that a woman came into the floor," he instructed quietly.

"Of course, my Lord," Ezra promised, bowing his head slightly in acknowledgement.

As the others began to stir, no one save Ezra, Boaz, and Ruth were aware of the proposal that had taken place in the still of the night. Even Mary was oblivious to what had happened. It did not take long once the sun was up for everyone to begin to disperse to their homes and soon only Mary, Ruth, Ezra, and Boaz remained on the threshing floor.

Mary knew she had missed something when Boaz approached Ruth, taking her hands in his. Ruth spoke first.

"Are you certain there is another kinsman nearer to me than you?" she asked nervously. "Naomi had said there was not even one, and now you are telling me there are two, yourself and one other?"

"I am certain," he answered apologetically. "The man is aged and has been sickly throughout his life. It was rumored that he had passed, so at the beginning of the wheat harvest, I traveled to his home just outside our city walls to learn the truth," he explained. "I saw him outside his home, he looked well at the time. I lost my nerve and refrained from speaking to him at that time." He smiled to her gently before continuing his confession. "With Mahlon's passing continuing to weigh on you, and with the difference in our age, I convinced myself you would not entertain a life with me at any rate," he spoke truthfully, "and I would never pressure you to do so."

"Obviously, there would be no pressure," Ruth laughed quietly.

Her laugh did wonders for his heart, and Boaz silently petitioned Jehovah once again that his older uncle would relinquish his right to marry Ruth, giving him the freedom to do so. *"But what man in his right mind would,"* Boaz admitted sadly to himself.

"I will do everything I can to convince him to relinquish his birthright granting me permission to wed you," he promised her. His heart broke as tears once again filled her eyes. Ruth looked away from him, and her innocence and humility tore at his soul. He knew if the older man chose to claim his right that she would do what she should. She would do what was right in the sight of Jehovah and the law. She would obey them both and marry the other kinsman, paying honor and respect to the memory of her former husband, Mahlon. Yet, Boaz knew that was not something he would relinquish easily. He would do all he could to earn the right to have her as his own.

In the meantime, he would not send her away without hope and a promise. "Bring the vail that thou hast upon thee, and hold it," he instructed her.

Ruth moved immediately to retrieve the beautiful golden vail he had given her during the night. Until this morning she had not realized how beautiful it really was, the moonlight before shadowing its splendor in the darkness. The silky material was finer than any Ruth had ever seen, the golden color reminding her of the way the sun danced on the grain when she first met Boaz.

"This was to be yours at any rate," he smiled as she held it out to him.

"Are you certain, Boaz?" She asked in awe of such a gift. "I have never seen such a vail as beautiful and as fine as this," she spoke sincerely.

"Which still pales in comparison to the beautiful and fine woman who now holds it in her possession," he answered with hesitation. "This vail," he spoke as he motioned to the scarlet fabric around his waist, "is something my mother cherished her entire life. It was a comfort to me in my childhood and continues to be a comfort to me now," he spoke honestly. "It is my hope and my prayer that this vail will be cherished by my bride and by our children in time to come."

"But Boaz, we do not yet know the wishes of the other kinsman," she began as he interrupted her by holding up his hand.

"The vail is yours to keep regardless of the outcome," he said looking into her eyes, "as is my heart. Cherish it always," and Ruth recognized the statement that he made was more of a question.

She smiled and nodded her head gently as he began scooping up the freshly winnowed barley.

Into the vail he measured six measures of barley, folded it into a sack and laid it upon her back. Before he sent her to her home, he had one more profession to make. He turned her to face himself as he continued.

"It is a business day, and the old man will likely be within the city gates this day. I will go this morning and seek him out. I will do everything in my power to convince him to relinquish his birth right to me. Take this barley and this vail to your home and wait there until I send word. And, Ruth," he said looking deep into her eyes, "do not doubt for a second that the weight upon your shoulders is nothing compared to my fondness and adoration of you." Boaz bent down and in the most genuine and tender form of affection he possessed, softly kissed her cheek. "If this goes poorly and I fail to receive his permission to possess his birthright and marry you, this vail will always remind you of my love," he spoke quietly. Ruth could not stop the tear which rolled along her face as she turned and walked away.

Her heart held a tirade of emotions as she began her walk home. She worked to still her mind and to think rationally about the events of the past few months. She had left her home in Moab after losing her husband tragically. She had journeyed across the desert, crossing both a mountain and a river to reach a place she had never been in a land where she was not wanted. She had been offended, ridiculed, and slightly abused while remaining as humble as she possibly could, all the while begging for food from someone who had been a perfect stranger.

She slowed her pace and her heart as that thought played in her head. "*Someone who had been a perfect stranger*," she thought. That "perfect stranger" had treated her like a queen from the moment he met her. That "perfect stranger" had gone above and beyond the realms of duty to provide for and assist her, and that "perfect stranger" had caused her to fall deeply in love with him, and it was all because…. he loves her too. She could not stop the smile that crossed her face as the realization finally reached her heart that Boaz had not been treating her with kindness for the sake of Elimelech; he had been treating her with kindness because of his love for her.

"And now there is ANOTHER kinsman," she thought aloud! Suddenly Jehovah spoke peace to her heart. Ruth was almost home, and Naomi would be eager to know what was happening. If Ruth arrived disgruntled and upset, Naomi would feel as if it was her fault for suggesting Ruth go to the threshing floor to begin with. Boaz was again doing something for her that was beyond his requirement to do. He was seeking out this "other kinsman," and Ruth knew without a doubt that he would do everything in his power to fight for the right to marry her himself.

She had barely crested the knoll when Naomi came running to meet her.

"Who art thou, my daughter?" she cried as she ran. "Did something go wrong?" she asked, clearly not expecting to see Ruth return alone. "Did he reject you as your kinsman redeemer?" she finally asked.

Ruth stilled the old woman as she reached her. "It is I, Naomi, the same Ruth as when I left last night, but it is well," she promised hugging the old woman. "Come inside, and I will tell you all, but I must get this load from my shoulders," she admitted.

Naomi was not sure if the load to which she referred was the physical load she carried, or the mental load she bore, but once she saw the amount of grain, and the beautiful vail in which it was wrapped, she was eager to hear the entire story, from beginning to end. Ruth left nothing out and told her everything. When she finished, Naomi stared at her, perplexed and in utter shock.

"There is another kinsman?" she questioned. "Word had come that he had passed," she stated when Ruth told her of Elimelech's younger brother.

"Boaz said as much," Ruth agreed, "and apparently at one time he had been very ill, but Boaz saw him just recently and is certain he is very much alive."

Naomi rose from the table where they sat, "Ruth, do you realize what this means?" she asked as tears rolled along her withered cheeks. "Orpah would have also had a kinsman redeemer. Jehovah had provided another, and I encouraged her to stay in that awful land when all along there were two. A redeemer for each of you."

Ruth listened to her mother-in-law and sympathized with her. She was correct in all she had said. Naomi had allowed her bitterness and a broken heart to cloud her judgement, and in doing so, she had forgotten what she had always taught her daughters-in-law, that Jehovah would always provide for their needs.

Immediately, the women did the only thing they could do. They knelt in the floor, bowing their heads, and prayed together. They prayed for Orpah back in Moab, they prayed for forgiveness for themselves once again, for all the ways they had failed Jehovah. And they prayed for Boaz to be diligent in his quest, to find the other kinsman and to convince him to relinquish his birthright allowing Boaz to marry Ruth, and for them to be allowed a lifetime of happiness.

When they finished, both ladies rose with quieted hearts. Ruth moved to the load she had deposited on the table.

"These six measures of barley he gave me; for he said to me, Go not empty into thy mother-in-law," she smiled as she unwrapped the vail.

Naomi chuckled. "Apparently, he is not angry with me for not divulging the information to you earlier that he is our next kinsman," she laughed. "All I wanted was for the two of you to find love. You deserve it so, Ruth," she smiled stroking the younger woman's face. "This vail is exquisite," Naomi continued, rubbing the material between her fingers.

Ruth smiled as she remembered what Boaz had said to her when he told her the vail was hers to keep.

"He told me that this vail was to be mine either way," she smiled staring at the beautiful creation. "He said that if his conversation with his uncle did not go in a way which to please him, that this vail would always remind me of his love for me." Ruth brushed a tear from her cheek.

"Sit still, my daughter until thou know how the matter will fall," Naomi comforted her as she placed her arms around the younger woman's shoulders, "for the man will not be in rest, until he have finished the thing this day."

Chapter Twenty

Boaz began his journey into town as soon as Ruth had left his sight. Ezra accompanied him, and on the way there, Boaz filled his most trusted companion in on all that had transpired.

"You are her next kinsman?" Ezra asked in unbelief. "What a perfect scenario," he laughed. "You fall for the woman, and then realize that you have every right to marry her, even though she is a Moabitess."

"Not every right," Boaz explained as they walked. "It depends upon this meeting in town today. I have to convince my uncle to give his birthright to me. But what man in his right mind would pass on such a woman?" Boaz asked sincerely.

"One who does not know the kind of woman she is," Ezra spoke truthfully. "I admit, when I first noticed your interest in Ruth, I was worried about the impact such a union could have on your business. She is a Moabitess, and that still does not sit kindly with some in our village.

As I got to know the true woman she is, however, I realized that her place of nativity would not matter to the people who do. She is a genuine soul, and I would be honored to work under her if she is to wed my employer and my dearest friend," Ezra said seriously. "I am a bit surprised you did not ask her to come with you this day," he admitted. "Is it not custom for the woman to accompany the man when it is she who is being spoken of?" he asked sincerely.

"Custom perhaps, but it is not law," Boaz clarified. "Ruth has been through enough; I would not intently subject her to more abuse. If he rejects her, which is honestly my prayer," he admitted, "she would never be haughty enough to do what would be expected of her, to spit upon his face. And why have her witness unnecessary rejection and humility," he finished. Ezra understood his thoughts completely.

As the men approached the city gate, Boaz turned to his companion. "Pray with me friend," he instructed Ezra as his heart thundered within his chest, "for words of wisdom and for peace, whatever the outcome."

"May Jehovah's will be done," Ezra agreed. The men prayed a quick prayer together and then moved into the city. Boaz took a seat right inside the city gate, watching as many came and went.

There was apparently much business to be done today, and the streets were crowded both with those who made legal transactions and those who were there to take care of other matters of legal business. Boaz and Ezra made small talk with those around them, not an unusual occurrence, while keeping a watchful eye for the one person Boaz was most eager to see. They talked of the prosperous crops, the blessing Jehovah had provided, and of future plans Boaz had to expand his fields and to increase his fortune.

The morning had grown long before the man Boaz had been longing to see came into view. Boaz jumped suddenly to his feet, interrupting the older man who was currently speaking, and immediately apologized for his lack of manners, but excused himself quickly, nonetheless. That his action caught the attention of those around him was an understatement, each of the men rising to their own feet to view whatever interaction was about to take place.

Boaz, so eager to gain the older kinsmen's attention, completely lost his senses. For the life of him, he could not remember the man's name, which until this moment, he had known his entire life as well as his own. Finally, afraid his moment would pass, he yelled the only phrase that would come to his mind.

"Ho, such a one!" he yelled gaining the attention of many at the gate. Man after man turned their attention to Boaz, while Ezra lowered his head into his hands hiding his smile, and his surprise, over the actions of his leader. He had never seen Boaz completely befuddled. This man whom he admired for his constant composure and mannerisms day after day, had completely forgotten the name of his nearest kinsman.

"Boaz!" the man called back to him extending his arm in salutation. "It is a pleasure to see you!"

"Come!" Boaz instructed, "Turn aside and sit down here," he motioned to where he had been sitting with Ezra. As they moved to the circle of business, Boaz pulled ten more elders of the city into their presence. "Sit ye down here," he beckoned, and the ten elders took places among them.

As the older kinsman approached, he noticed Boaz, Ezra and the ten elders of the city, all gathered into a circle.

"I assume this is more than a friendly conversation, nephew?" he asked as he saluted the others around him and took a seat. "What manner of meeting is this?" he asked in confusion.

"It is a matter of business, uncle," Boaz began. Then with a final prayer for the right words to say, he began.

"Naomi, that is come again out of the country of Moab, selleth a parcel of land, which was our brother Elimelech's." Boaz stilled his heart when he noticed the immediate interest on the face of his uncle. Unfortunately, at this point, he was clearly interested in claiming his birthright. "And I thought to advertise thee," Boaz continued, "Buy it before the inhabitants, and before the elders of my people. If thou wilt redeem it, redeem it: but if thou wilt not redeem it, then tell me, that I may know: for there is none to redeem it beside thee; and I am after thee."

His uncle shook his head and with barely a moment's hesitation the words Boaz had feared became a reality.

"I will redeem it," he acknowledged slapping his thigh and making a move to stand considering the deal closed.

Boaz held up his hand to stop him. The man stalled and reclaimed his seat. Ezra smiled to himself knowing what his employer was up to; the other elders of the city looked around at one another, clearly as confused as the old uncle.

"What day thou buyest the field of the hand of Naomi," Boaz continued, "thou must buy it also of Ruth the Moabitess, the wife of the dead, to raise up the name of the dead upon his inheritance," he finished absolutely.

Sudden surprise was evident on the older man's face. The uncle looked at Boaz in shock and disgust. "A Moabitess?" he questioned. "What meanest thou this?" he asked, as even speaking the word left a taste of bitterness upon his lips.

"Aye," Boaz continued, "You cannot purchase the land from Naomi without also agreeing to redeem the widow, Ruth, who was married to her son, Mahlon, and returned with her from the land of Moab. It is all, or nothing, as you know, Uncle," Boaz finished respectfully. The elders of the city turned their attention to the old man, and the excited prospect of purchasing the land fell from his face. As the old man's face turned to stone, Boaz felt as if his heart had taken flight. He worked to retain his composure though inside himself he wanted to shout.

"I cannot redeem it for myself, lest I mar mine own inheritance," the uncle fumed. Boaz struggled for a moment as he listened, between wanting to thank the man for the words he knew were about to come, and at the same time longing to punch him for the insult cast toward his new bride.

"Redeem thou my right to thyself; for I cannot redeem it," he finished spitting upon the ground. His rudeness repulsed Boaz, but for the sake of retaining his own happiness, he let it go as his uncle reached down to unloose his sandal. He slapped the shoe into the hand of Boaz, therefore, in the presence of all the elders gathered, relinquishing his birthright to the land of Elimelech, and allowing Boaz to act as kinsman redeemer to Ruth.

Boaz watched as the old man hobbled away, one foot bare, muttering to himself as he went. For a moment, Boaz felt sorry for the old man who had come into town that day having no idea he would be returning home with such news as he had learned, and lost. All because of his pride and prejudices toward a woman he did not even know. But his sorrow for the ignorant fool was fleeting, for he had won the right to marry Ruth.

He could not stop the smile that overspread his face as he spoke to the elders still in his presence, and all those who had gathered at the site anxious to see what all the fuss was about.

"Ye are witnesses this day," he shouted so that all in his earshot could hear him, "that I have bought all that was Elimelech's, and all that was Chilion's and Mahlon's, of the hand of Naomi. Moreover. Ruth the Moabitess, the wife of Mahlon, have I purchased to be my wife, to raise up the name of the dead upon his inheritance, that the name of the dead be not cut off from among his brethren, and from the gate of his place: ye are witnesses this day," he stated again as he held the shoe proudly in the air, making sure everyone knew that she was rightfully and legally his to claim.

Ezra led the "hoorah" that followed. Once the crowd had silenced, the elders began to congratulate and speak to Boaz at once, all seemingly as excited as he over his accomplishment, none caring at the moment that Boaz, one of the wealthiest men in town, would be wed to a Moabite woman.

"We are witnesses," they agreed. "The lord make the woman that is come into thine house like Rachel and like Leah, which two did build the house of Israel: and do thou worthily in Ephratah, and be famous in Bethlehem: And let thy house be like the house of Pharez, whom Tamar bare unto Judah, of the seed which the Lord shall give thee of this young woman."

Boaz was met by more cheers and claps on the back as he left the city gates with Ezra by his side and the shoe clasped firmly in his hand.

Jehovah had blessed him once again this day. Ezra did not have to ask his leader where their next stop would be as the two of them all but ran out of the city.

Chapter Twenty-One

Ruth busied herself throughout the morning with daily chores and then by storing the barley Boaz had once again provided. She tried not to let her mind wander to the events she assumed were taking place in town. She had no idea who the man was that Boaz would be speaking to, and she surely had no idea how the business proposal would go, but what she did know, and what brought peace to her troubled mind, was that Jehovah was in control. No matter how the events transpired and ended, He would be with her, and He already knew exactly what the outcome would be.

She moved out of doors a little after the noon hour feeling as if the fresh air of the day would do her good. She found herself in a spot that she had come to love, the area behind the barn that overlooked the meadow, now bursting with wild flowers that blew gently in the cool breeze. She could sink among the flowers and be almost undetected here, allowing her mind, and her emotions, to wander freely.

When they had first moved to Bethlehem, Ruth would come here when she needed space from Naomi, from the world. To pray, to cry, to give herself time to think back to Moab when she still had a husband. She could not help but smile at the thought of him even now, her first love. She would never forget Mahlon. Were it not for him and his family, she may never have been led to Jehovah, and she certainly would not have found a home in Bethlehem. But she had soon realized, as she sat in her thoughtful place, that her thoughts would lead less often to Mahlon now and most often to Boaz.

She no longer felt as if she were dishonoring the memory of her former husband, for she had not and would not ever stop loving him, she had simply made room in her heart to love another. Mahlon had no need of her now, he was gone. Boaz did need her, and he was here in the present time, and most importantly, as she had recently come to realize, Boaz loved her too. He did not care that she had been married and was left a penniless widow with nothing to offer save herself; he did not care that she was a Moabitess and had come from a forbidden, foreign land. And apparently, though they had never spoken of it, he did not care that she was apparently barren. In the eyes of the world, she was completely worthless, but Boaz saw something in her that she could not even see in herself, and he chose to love her regardless of her failures.

The thought brought a heaviness to her heart. Would Boaz continue to love her once he realized there was a great probability that she could never give him a child? She had never conceived with Mahlon; what were the possibilities that she could conceive at all? Would she bring shame to Boaz were he to marry her? The fact that he would be marrying a Moabitess was a mark against him already, perhaps that fact would eventually be overlooked due to his obligation to marrying her as a kinsmen redeemer, but were she to remain barren after their union would she bring further dishonor to his name?

This thought had not occurred to Ruth until now, so as she had so often done in recent days she took her petition to Jehovah. This time, however, though still reverent, she did not bow her head. She simply sank to her knees and looked to the sky as she spoke the words aloud.

"Jehovah," she began looking beyond the clouds overhead, "I come to you again to find solace at your feet, knowing not the plans you have for me, but knowing whatever they are that they will be in the best interest for all involved. You have brought me from a desolate place Lord, a place of nothing, to a place where all my hope lies in you. Once again, I have met the most wonderful man, Jehovah. A man that I know you directed me to. He is so kind and so good and has provided for me and for Naomi so much that we have no fear of going hungry before the next harvest, and Lord, I thank you, once again, for that.

"I know that marriage to a kinsman redeemer seems to be the only hope for a future for two poor widows, yet, Lord, I have been fortunate, not to have found love once, in Mahlon, but now to have found love again, in Boaz, and he is a kinsman! But Lord, as you know, there is another. There is another man who is eligible to perform the role of my kinsman redeemer. I know not who he is, but I know that you have him here for a purpose. And if that purpose is to be a redeemer for me, then let it be.

"I cannot hide, nor do I desire to hide from you, the fact that I do love Boaz and that my selfish request is that I be allowed a future with him, and not with this other man. However, I do not wish to bring shame to Boaz. I do not know if I can bear children; I do not know if my being a Moabitess would hinder his business. I do not know if I can live up to the expectations of the people here; I only know that I love him. But I also know that You love him more, so Lord, please do what is best for him. Allow however the events unfold in town this day to be what is best for Boaz.

"You have already done so much for me, Lord, I ask that you please move in a way that will bring Boaz the peace and happiness that he so much deserves. I would rather live a desolate and poor life for the rest of my days than to be displeasing to You or to bring sorrow to the house of Boaz. So, Lord, please, over my selfish desires, please grant Boaz what he needs, for Lord, I know that You know best. Thy will be done, and not my own," she finished.

So intent was she in her prayer, that Ruth did not realize she had been joined in her meadow. Boaz had come upon her and remained silent until she finished her prayer, not meaning to eavesdrop but being fascinated once again by the humble and unselfish thoughts and prayers of this miraculous woman. He made no movement, no sound, until Ruth stood and turned to face him.

She stood silent as he took the few steps necessary to reach her then gently raised his hands to frame her face, wiping the trail of tears from her cheeks with his thumbs. Neither spoke a word as Boaz looked into her eyes, then lowered his lips to touch hers. It was a simple kiss, a gentle token of love and affection, so simple in fact, that Ruth was certain it was a kiss goodbye, forever to be known only to them and to God, and never to be spoken of again. Sorrow filled her heart.

Boaz released her face though his eyes never left hers and slowly reached into his pocket. When she broke his gaze, it was to look into his open hand extended before her containing a small handful of olives. And then he smiled. His smile spread from ear to ear, and joy radiated from his eyes in such a way that she knew Jehovah had heard and answered their prayers in her favor.

"If Jehovah blesses our home with children, then what joy shall come to our home! But if He does not, then so-be-it," he continued quietly, "for you will be there, and never have I experienced such joy." He pulled her close again and this time he kissed her so fervently that she pulled away in laughter.

"Is it true?" she asked as he joined in her glee. "Am I allowed to be so happy once again?" she asked. Boaz had wrapped his arms around her waist and refused to let her go.

"Yes, my sweet Ruth, it is true," he beamed. "I have purchased the birthright from my uncle, and we will be wed at once. You will come with me this night, never to be separated from me again, lest Jehovah God chooses to do so."

Before she could speak, Boaz bent low and scooped her into his arms, carrying her effortlessly across the field back to the home where Naomi and Ezra waited.

"My precious daughter," the old woman crooned as she held Ruth close just a few minutes later. "Blessed be Jehovah who hath loaded you with benefits," she cried. "Such joy that has come back into this house, but oh, how I shall miss you," she finished, caressing the younger woman's face.

"Miss her you shall not, Naomi," Boaz spoke from his place behind his bride. "You shall come with us," he instructed. "Or we shall come to you," he continued. "I care not where we live," he went on, "but live as one family we shall," he insisted.

"This land is yours now, Boaz," Naomi reminded him. "I shall be content in the fact that you and Ruth are together," she smiled. "And there are plenty of fields to be planted!" she reminded him. Ruth recognized that smile, the smile that she had not seen on Naomi's face in years since the time Elimelech had become ill in Moab. How Ruth had missed the sweet, smiling face of her mother-in-law. It brought her such joy to see it once again.

The four of them stood together in the main living quarters of the house, laughing and rejoicing over the news Boaz had brought. They made plans for a quick wedding to take place, for Boaz was determined not to part from his new bride. The wedding would take place that very day, with a proper celebration to follow a few days after. Everyone was in agreement and late that afternoon, Boaz and Ruth were wed in the field where Boaz had first looked upon Ruth with such empathy and compassion.

The celebration that was held a few days after the wedding was a truly massive affair with music and dancing, food, and delicacies only a few had ever tasted. The event was the talk of Bethlehem for years to come, for Boaz extended the celebration to everyone, clearly intent on showing off his new bride.

Ezra and Mary announced that Ezra and her father had come to an agreement, and they too would be wed the following spring. Lydia and

Samuel were also in attendance, now recently wed, along with Abigail and Jedidiah, all so happy for the newly married Ruth and Boaz that they could hardly contain their excitement.

Ruth could honestly say that at that moment, she had never been so happy. Her life with Mahlon had been a good one, but it had been in Moab, the godless place of her youth. Now, she truly felt she was home, in the land of Israel, God's chosen nation, with a man who loved her more than life itself.

A few short months later, Boaz settled himself in his favorite spot, late one evening, a fire crackling in front of him. He breathed in the night air, so content and satisfied with his life that he almost felt guilty. Naomi had retired to her quarters for the evening, and Ruth was finishing up something inside the house before joining him outdoors, as had become their nightly ritual.

The night was quiet and the stars shone brightly overhead when his wife came to his side, kneeling at his feet.

"Come closer, my love," he instructed reaching for her.

"I am quite content, here," she spoke though she moved to do his bidding.

He opened his arms to her, and she settled against his chest, both of them gazing at the array of stars overhead.

"Jehovah paints such an amazing picture," he spoke softly watching the stars as they twinkled overhead.

"Hmmm, that he does," she agreed. "Do you ever feel guilty for being so blessed," Ruth questioned him, the back of her head still lying on his chest.

"I suppose, I do," he answered honestly. "For what more could I ask than for all He has already given," he finished.

"A healthy child, perhaps," Ruth answered. Boaz moved her, turning her to face him.

"I have told you, Ruth, I am content with the blessings we have already been given. I am content just having you in my life. If Jehovah has children in our future that will indeed be another blessing, but if he does not…"

"I am with child," she interrupted him. He stopped speaking, staring speechless into her face.

"What?" he finally asked, begging her to repeat the words again.

"I am with child," she beamed.

"Are you sure," he asked as he pulled her into an embrace. "Are you well?" he asked releasing his hold on her and looking into her eyes.

She laughed before answering him. Her laughter still taking his breath away.

"I am quite certain. I shared my suspicions with Naomi just today, and she agreed the signs are all there," she acknowledged as he pulled her carefully to himself once again.

"I cannot contain my joy!" he yelled, loud enough for the world to hear. Ruth laughed, thankful that no one was within hearing distance, other than Naomi, who now came running from the house rejoicing at the news Ruth had shared.

The three laughed together, wept together and then knelt to give thanks together. Each of their lives had been impacted in ways that could point only to Jehovah. Each of them had hope once again in ways that could point only to Jehovah. And each of them would forever tell their story of the peace, restoration, redemption, and grace that could only be found in Jehovah where they rested and they trusted—at His feet.

Closing Thoughts

Peace that passes all understanding is found, At His Feet.

Complete restoration is found, At His Feet.

Grace is found, At His Feet.

Redemption is found, At His Feet.

Mercy is found, At His Feet.

Salvation is found, At His Feet.

There is nothing that cannot be found at the feet of our precious Lord and Savior, Jesus Christ. The story of Boaz and Ruth is a story of redemption, and it so mirrors the story of our Kinsman Redeemer, Jesus Christ. However, where Ruth had another possibility of redemption through a second Kinsman Redeemer, we only have one. Jesus Christ.

"Jesus saith unto him, I am the way, the truth, and the life: no man cometh unto the Father, but by me." John 14:6. KJV

We had no hope. There was no way. We had no future, until Jesus Christ gave Himself for us. We were destined for an eternal life in hell, but Jesus came and made a way for us to live with Him forever in Heaven. If you will trust Him, He will completely provide for your future on earth, and He provides for your future in eternity.

Find everything you need and more, At His Feet.

Other books in this Series.

The Prudent Queen

When Angels Speak

We Have Heard

Made in the USA
Columbia, SC
25 April 2023